AN NSB WEDDING

An NSB Novel By
Alyson Santos

D1519478

This novel is a work of fiction and intended for mature readers. Events and persons depicted are of a fictional nature and use language, make choices, and face situations inappropriate for younger readers.

Names, characters, places and events are the product of the author's imagination. Any resemblance to actual events, locations, organizations, or people, living or dead, is entirely coincidental and not intended by the author.

Cover Design by Adam Shook/L. Woods

ISBN-13: 978-1791991050

Prologue: Eighteen Months Earlier
Suite 403

It could be going worse, I guess. Luke let me into his hotel room which was more than I expected when I knocked. A scowl, a slam, maybe even a direct fist blow, and yet I got none of the above. Nope, just some brief wave of recognition followed by a resigned sigh. He stepped back so I could enter, and that was the extent of the reunion.

We've kept it pretty safe so far. He doesn't say much anyway, so it's not hard. Mostly he just tracks a wear pattern from the couch to the minibar. At least he's getting exercise? Damn, he looks bad—except when he talks about her.

"You staying over tonight, Case?" he asks, draining his glass.

Surprised, I glance at him to get a read of the offer. Is that sarcasm? There's no humor in his expression though. Not much of anything, really, just exhaustion. Yes, that's it. He looks flat-out depleted.

"Sure, if that's okay."

He shrugs. "We can grab breakfast tomorrow before you go."

"With your new girlfriend?"

I regret my joke the second it comes out. His gaze lowers, zero hint of a smile.

"It's not like that, man. I told you."

"I know. Sorry. She sounds great."

"Callie is… special. She sees you, ya know?"

So he's said. Several times. Still, seems like a stretch. I get that he's grasping but some random chick in a diner?

"And the fact that you're Luke Craven of Night Shifts Black has nothing to do with her interest?" Sorry, but someone has to say it, and even if I'm not the best man for the job, I'm the only one apparently.

"That's just it. She had no clue."

"Really?" I try to keep my skepticism out of the equation. I've pushed him pretty far already.

"I'm telling you, dude. She's different. Even when she found out who I was, it didn't change anything. I'm still just Luke, and she's just Callie."

"Huh." Okay, maybe I'm a little intrigued. Still not sure I trust this chick, but there's no doubt she's accomplished in a few days what we couldn't do in months. Luke's eyes change when he talks about her. The light flickers back for the briefest of seconds and gives a glimpse of what he could be. It fades just as quickly, but it's enough to make me think a breakfast to check things out is probably a good idea. Last thing we need right now is some gold-digger taking advantage of his vulnerable state.

"She's a pistol too. You wouldn't guess it at first. She's so sweet and genuine, but then bam, she'll smack you with a one-liner that just rips the rug out."

I smile to myself. Sounds more like my type than his.

"You'll love her, Case. She could definitely handle you."

Is he reading my mind? He always could. A virtual brother thing, and one of the biggest gaps in my life since he left. Funny how much we miss what's right in front of us.

I lean back on the couch with a smirk. "Handle me? I need to be handled?"

"Uh, yeah, dude. If that thing with Jana was any indication."

"Eh, that's over. Again."

"Exactly."

Fair enough.

"So you want me to go to breakfast to hang out with you or to meet my future girlfriend?" I tease.

He thinks for a moment, a rare smile spreading over his lips. "Casey and Callie. Kind of has a ring to it, no?"

Maybe I will stay for breakfast. What could a few eggs and toast hurt? I'll need to eat before hitting the road anyway. Besides, I can count on one finger the number of times Luke has tried to set me up with a woman.

One: Callie, the breakfast club girl.

I'll admit, he's got my attention. Yep, this should be interesting.

1: Tuesday 8:06pm, 4 Days

"Everyone good?" I scan my bandmates from behind my drum kit, looking for any sign that we need to run something again. Man, I hope not. After two weeks of tour rehearsals, I'm ready to crash. It's not like I have the wedding of the century coming up or anything. Oh wait.

"Hey, Case. Thanks for sticking with us as MD," Luke says, falling into stride as we make our way to catering. "I know you have a lot on your plate."

"Not a problem. Getting married doesn't make me a shitty music director."

Luke smirks and bumps my shoulder as we walk. "You know what I mean. You ready for this?"

"Which? The world tour or spending the rest of my life with your best friend?"

"You're my best friend."

"Fine. Second best friend."

"Marriage, dude. Touring's the only thing you're good at."

"Fuck off," I laugh, but my smile fades. Am I ready? I mean, I was ready to marry Callie Roland the day I met her in that little café. So what just tightened in my chest? Can you be *too* ready to marry someone?

"Hey bro, that was supposed to be an easy question." Luke's quick study of my face belies the humor in his tone.

I force a smile. "I'm a hundred percent ready to see you in your bridesmaid's dress."

"Ha. Don't worry. Callie's letting me wear a tux even though I'm standing up for both of you." The concern returns to his face, the questions, and I pretend not to notice as we approach the makeshift green room where our girls are waiting for us.

Well, *waiting* may be generous. Callie, Holland, and Mila have been inseparable since rehearsals for our joint NSB and Limelight tour forced us into 24/7 bonding. We're practically standing in their laughing cluster before they notice us.

"Hey, hon!" If there's ever a moment you want to hang onto, it's the look on Callie's face when she sees me. That inner chest-clench returns.

"Hey, babe." I draw her in for a kiss, and my body doesn't give a shit about our audience. All it remembers is that our crazy schedules have kept us apart for too long.

"You're sweaty," she whispers.

"Yeah, sorry. The lights and stuff."

"I know. It's sexy."

My eyes shoot to hers. She's not exactly the flirty, PDA type. "Really? Interesting." Cue adrenaline. Cue… *that*.

A smile teases her lips when she notices me harden against her hips. Where did this minx come from?

"Maybe I've been missing you lately. A lot," she says, gaze moving down my chest and landing on the zipper of my jeans. I pull her tighter, erasing the rest of the distance between us so she can feel more of my response and suffer with me. Her exhale leaves a hot impression on my shoulder, and I swear it burns my skin.

"You, me, hotel room, now," I growl against her ear.

She locks her arms around my waist, forcing us into painful alignment. I'm not an impatient man, but this?

"Get a room," Luke calls over, his arm tucked around Holland. Jesse and Mila are wrapped up as well. You'd think we've been on the road for a month, not down the hall for six hours. Eli, Sweeny, and the rest of the Limelight guys are enamored with the snack table.

"We intend to," I call back, leading—yanking?—my girl to the exit. "Catch you later."

"Uh." Luke points to the clock on the wall.

"What?"

"Kenneth wants to review final notes in fifteen minutes, and then we have the WHTX interview."

"Fuck."

"Language," Callie says. I give her a glare that she returns with a not-so-innocent smile. "Oh well. Guess I'm on my own again tonight."

"Can't we reschedule?" I ask Luke.

"You mean, for after we tear down and roll out tonight so you can get to your wedding extravaganza?"

"Fuck!" I run a hand through my hair and send an apologetic look to Callie.

Her smirk melts into compassion, which is ten times worse. She knows how much I'm hurting at this point. It's pure torture the way she licks her lips. Exposes her neck with a tug of her hair down her back. I trace my thumb over her skin, and her lids flutter closed. Maybe she's hurting too. Am I an asshole to hope so?

"I can try to stay awake?" she whispers, and I let out a long sigh. She'd do it too because with Callie, everyone else comes first.

S'why it's my job to take care of the world's caretaker.

"No, babe. We'll be late tonight. Get some sleep." I lean down for a quick kiss and don't dare to let it deepen.

"Less than a week, Case." Huge gorgeous eyes turn up to me, brimming with anticipation. Love. Hope. Lust. Possession. All the things I want to abduct back to our hotel and ravage until she's the one locking us in the room and blowing off responsibilities. Blowing off.

Stop it, Casey.

I glance back at the guys. "Maybe I should quit the band," I mutter.

"On what grounds? Horniness? Seems short-sighted," she says.

"Hey, there's nothing *short* about my horniness."

Her grin is almost too much to bear. "Okay, fine. And then do what with your life?"

"I don't know. Be your sex slave?"

She laughs "Yeah? How well does that pay?"

"I don't know. What are you offering?"

"Depends. Would you finally give in to getting a cat?"

"Those are your terms?"

"Two cats."

"Two?"

"No wait, three."

"You're impossible."

She plants a kiss on my lips. "Have fun with your band stuff. I'll see you later, hun. Maybe I'll sleep naked just in case."

How can an angel be so evil?

Holland and Mila are waiting for her, and blow air kisses at us.

"Newlyweds," Eli mumbles behind me.

2: WEDNESDAY 5:53PM, 3 DAYS

Callie wasn't awake when I finally got back to the room last night. She mumbled something about rainforests. Or carparks? And I couldn't bring myself to wake her up. Thankfully, she was also joking about the naked sleeping, and I managed to keep my dick under control as I drew her into my arms. Who knew being with the person you loved could be almost as hard as being away from them?

Now, we've just checked into our new hotel after another brutal leg of travel. At least we get to camp out in one location for a few days. If all goes well, we won't have to do anything other than show our faces at some wedding events and greet incoming guests. After this past month, I'm looking forward to much needed R&R with Callie, especially since our tour will push the honeymoon into next year. Endless hours of romantic bliss coming up, and I plan to soak in every second. Funny that I'm feeling the pressure of time when we're preparing for a lifetime together, but that's musician life for you.

All hope of an evening naked with the most beautiful woman on the planet is dashed when the most annoying woman comes rushing toward us in the lobby.

"There's the happy couple!"

"Rita, hi." Callie is all smiles and hugs for our wedding coordinator. I'm all impatient nod.

"I've taken the liberty of putting together a schedule of events for your stay. It includes the locations for all the receptions, meals, and—"

"Wait, receptions?" I ask.

"Well, yes. Every morning we'll have a formal brunch to welcome the guests who arrived the previous day, and—"

"Wait. Huh?"

"The Welcome Brunch." She says it like she didn't just make that up right this second.

"No."

"What do you mean, no?" she quips, painted eyebrows lifting high on her forehead.

"I mean, no. Is that even a thing?"

Callie reaches for my hand. "Hun…"

Nope, too pissed even for Callie-calm. But Rita doesn't flinch. She hasn't since the day we started choosing napkin shapes and shit. Pretty sure that's why Callie insisted on keeping her around.

"If you recall, it's just a brunch-style event each morning. You'll have to eat anyway, so it works perfectly."

Not when you want to be naked in bed with your fiancée.

"I just can't— You know what? Fine. Whatever. Look, we're tired. Can we just go over the rest tomorrow?"

Her face scrunches into a painful display of sympathy. Must not have covered that expression in wedding-planner school. "Ooh… Well, I wish that were possible. But unfortunately, if you *look at the schedule*, you'll see you have a Welcoming Dinner in just over an hour."

"Welcoming dinner? I thought it was a morning brunch."

"That's something else. This is the Welcoming *Dinner*."

"Who the hell are we welcoming?"

Callie shoves an elbow into my side. Sorry, but what level of wedding hell is this?

"*You're* being welcomed."

"Huh?"

"It's a reception to honor—"

"Well, can't we be *welcomed* tomorrow?"

She looks like I just suggested serving baby unicorn steaks. "I'm afraid that's not possible. Preparations for The Welcoming Dinner are already underway. We're scheduled for forty-eight guests."

"You're just making shit up. No way that's a thing." I shoot an exasperated look at Callie. "That can't be a thing, babe."

Callie sighs and soothes my fist between her palms. "I know, sweetie. It's a lot, but remember your brothers and sisters are coming in to help out, and we thought it would be good to greet them all at once tonight rather than try to meet up."

"So this *is* a welcoming brunch!"

"It's dinner," Rita corrects. "Starts at seven pm. Mediterranean fare."

I glare over at her. "I don't want to fucking welcome anyone. I just want to sleep. We haven't had a break in weeks."

Horrified at my lack of wedding hospitality etiquette, Rita sends a pleading look to Callie. Oh hell no. She does not get to force my fiancée between us.

"Fine. We'll be back down at *seven pm* to welcome the shit out of everyone. Welcome!" I call to the dude rolling a carryon bag toward the elevator. He looks back, confused, and I wave with my brightest smile.

"Welcome!" That's for the concerned grandma who tucks her grandchild to her side as she shuffles past. Callie tries to hold in a snicker beside me.

"There. See? I was born for this." I throw my arms up and wave to the lobby. "Welcome, everyone! Bienvenido! Aloha! Oi! Willkommen!" I give Rita a look, and Callie chuckles.

Rita appears ready to cry. "Clearly you need some time to unwind," she says. "We'll see you at dinner." She turns on an expensive black heel and stomps off to her imaginary Rosette and Champagne Kingdom.

"You're a jerk, Casey Barrett," Callie says, pushing me toward the elevator.

"I'm the jerk? What's with all the damn welcoming? If I'd known about this…"

I cringe, and her eyebrows lift in challenge.

"Yeah? If you'd known, then what?"

I draw her into the elevator and pull her back against my chest. "I would have kidnapped you and forced you to marry me in front of a judge," I whisper in her ear. "Then we'd be off on a beach somewhere sipping cocktails and making babies."

She giggles and relaxes into me. "What about your rehearsals?"

"Okay, fine. We'd be in a hotel room making babies."

"I thought you wanted to wait with kids."

"It's a fantasy, babe. Enjoy the dream."

She locks my arms around her. "Reality won't be so bad. We're just tired. By tomorrow we'll be more than ready to *welcome*."

"Hmm. People didn't seem to like that just now."

"Not strangers, silly." She turns to face me. "We got this."

"As long as I got you."

She grins and pulls my lips to hers. "Lame."

∞∞∞

"Oh my gosh, it's so beautiful!"

I follow Callie's gaze around our suite, and I gotta say, it's not bad. My mood shifts slightly into more positive territory. This hotel has "bridal suite" locked down. A few bouquets of flowers brighten the surfaces and, is that a gift basket? Callie is already investigating.

"I'm not sure when we'll have time for summer sausages, but it's a nice gesture," she says. I can see the thank you note to the hotel staff already forming in her head.

"It's probably for later. They know we'll need our strength for tonight's workout," I tease, wrapping my arms around her from behind. She giggles from my scruff against her neck.

"Nice try. Because first…" She twists around and ruins any hope I have of sexy time with a peck on the chin. "Welcoming Dinner."

So I might grunt at that… or pout… whatever. "Fine. Can we at least shower together quick? Just a little innocent fun, I promise."

Her expression is encouraging. The way her fingers dig into my biceps—definitely a good sign. I've just switched on the full-charm when—

"Eek!"

I spin around to track her death stare. "What?" I ask.

"Right there!"

"Where?"

"Right there!" She jumps back a good five feet.

"What's right there? A ghost? Burglar? What?"

"On the wall!"

I squint at the wall, as if the new perspective will give me some insight into chick-brain.

"Babe, I don't see anything."

"Next to the picture."

She's pressed against the foyer wall now, finger pointing with all the foreboding of the Ghost of Christmas Future. "Spider," she whispers, eyes full of impending doom.

"Cal, I don't…" I take a few steps toward the wall. Maybe there's a black spot to the right of the frame?

"This?" I point at the pin-prick of tiny legs.

"Yes!" She covers her mouth and takes more steps toward the exit. Soon she'll be in the hall.

I turn back to the intruder who's now ruined any chance I had of getting lucky. "Dude, you're so screwed," I mutter, slipping off my sneaker.

"No!" This scream is more hostile than the initial shriek. I turn, weapon suspended in mid-air.

"What?"

"Don't kill it!"

"Um…"

"It doesn't deserve to die!"

I glance at the bug. At my shoe. Back to Callie. "So you don't want it gone?"

"Of course I do!"

"You *do* want it gone?" I raise the shoe again.

"Gone, yes, not dead! Put it outside or something."

I swallow and pull in a deep breath. "Okay…"

"Here." She darts forward and disappears into the bathroom. Does she think spiders can jump twenty feet in one shot? I keep my research questions to myself as I wait.

She emerges seconds later and tosses me a cup from the bathroom.

I catch it against my chest. "Nice thought, but how do I get it in here? I doubt he's aware his options are the cup or death."

"Um…" She bites her lip, scanning the room. "Oh, got it." Grabbing the channel guide brochure, she legit slides it across the floor in my direction. It goes all of a foot.

We both stare at it for several seconds before I sigh and cross the room to pick it up.

"Love you, babe," she says with a grin. "Eek! It's moving! It's moving, hurry!"

How she can see that speck of dust move five millimeters in the dark from that distance, is beyond me. Must be some radar or sixth sense or something. I quicken my pace because I'm thinking there's nothing worse for a relationship than losing visual of a spider. On closer inspection, I guess it could be an entire centimeter closer to the frame on the wall? Lunging forward I trap the little dude with the cup like the superhero I am. After shoving the brochure between the cup and the wall, I verify I've won the battle and press the brochure on top to secure it.

"Okay, I have it trapped. Can you open the window?"

She nods slowly, clearly not wanting to move but knowing she's out of options with me on Spider Guard Duty. "Just stay there until I open it," she warns.

I try to keep a straight face and fight the ten-year-old in me who wants to pretend to throw it at her. Mom would be proud when I manage to stay put.

She pulls open the blinds and studies the glass. "I don't think it opens."

I scan the frame as well. "It probably doesn't. Hotel windows usually don't."

"Crap."

She crosses her arms and commits way more brain cells to this dilemma than can possibly be healthy.

"It's fine. I'll just flush it," I say, moving toward the bathroom with my prisoner.

"No!"

"Huh?"

"Casey, you can't!"

"Why not?"

"You'll kill it!"

"Well, yeah?"

"You can't kill it! It wasn't hurting anyone."

Shit, is she going to cry? Over a damn spider she hates? Even worse, it's the freaking cutest sight ever.

"Okaaaay?" Cute or not, I'm still at a loss. "What do you want me to do with it then?"

"Um…" Her teeth sink into her lip again as she considers. "I guess you'll have to take it down to the lobby and put it outside."

"What? No fucking way," I mumble.

"Language."

"Sorry, but come on. You want me to carry this thing down four stories, through the lobby, and out to the parking lot?"

"Well, not the parking lot. It might get run over. Maybe the flower bed? There'd be lots of places to build a web and plenty of food and maybe some friends...?"

Her grin is because she knows I'll follow her orders. Maybe one day I'll be able to resist her, but it's not looking good for this century. At least she has the courtesy of looking adorable when she bosses me around.

Even so, I'm pretty sure I'm growling on my way to the exit. She maintains a wide arc as I move across the room. Once I'm safely in the corridor, she hoists her suitcase onto the bed and starts unzipping it.

"You're not coming with me?" I ask.

She glances over, clearly surprised. "Are you kidding? Lock myself in a small moving box with that monster? Not a chance."

∞∞∞

"Hey, Case."

"Hey, Luke."

I glance at his cup as I step off the elevator. "Coffee?"

"Kind of. Some soy milk thing for Holland." He glances at mine. "Spider?"

I nod.

He nods back.

"Well, good luck," he says, moving past me into the elevator.

"You too, man. See you at dinner."

"Yup."

∞∞∞

I navigate the lobby like it's totally normal to walk around with a spider in a cup covered by a channel guide. I'm a firm believer that not showing fear is half the battle. The staff at the door seem a little more suspicious than the others I've passed, though, possibly because after saying hello I beeline for the flowerbed.

"Can I help you, sir?" A security guard asks before I reach the promised land. By *help* he clearly means *send you back where you came from* and *sir* is *crazy man with a spider in a cup.*

"Nope. Just taking care of business." Well, that certainly didn't help.

He raises a brow. "Sir, there are restrooms in the lobby."

I force a laugh and shake my head. "No, no. Not that kind of business. I have a spider." I hold up the channel-guide-cup-trap because… yeah.

"Sir, we'd ask you not to release wildlife on hotel property."

"Oh it's not wildlife. Just a spider." I bend down to get to work. This conversation is going nowhere.

"Sir, for the safety of the guests, please do not release your pet on our property." He's got a hand on the radio, ready for action. I already see the headlines. Rebel Rocker Unleashes Killer Spider Dot.

"Ha! No. It was on the wall in our room. I wanted to flush it but… never mind. Here, look."

He steps back when I approach with the cup outstretched. Still, he can't resist a peek and leans to unsafe levels in order to inspect my contraband. By his look, he's not impressed.

"Sir?"

I pull the cup back and—shit. "Um… Well there *was* a spider in here."

He nods, his expression shifting from irritation to pity. "Of course there was, sir. Have a nice evening."

"Thanks," I mutter and trudge back to the entrance. I'm careful to toss the empty cup in the trash bin. The last thing I need right now is a litter citation.

3: WEDNESDAY 7:04PM, 3 DAYS

People say marriage requires total honesty. Those people clearly aren't including the fate of spiders in that advice. So maybe instead of the truth I tell Callie her spider is happily nestled in a garden palace amidst an endless buffet of seasonal insects. Maybe she believes me and thanks me with a sweet kiss and promise to make up our intimate time the very first chance we get. Maybe it all makes me a terrible person, but we don't have time to find a new hotel if she learns the spider could still be haunting these hallways. Maybe that's why I'm now following her through a maze of resort amenities to the Crescent Moon Banquet Room where she's worried about being late and I'm worried about being a spider-killer. None of this helps my attitude toward Rita's Welcoming shit, and I do my best to suck back any remaining protests.

Yep, still skeptical this is actually a thing.

Callie reaches back and grabs my hand as we approach the ornately labeled *Banquet Room*, as if fearing she'll be entering alone in a second. I squeeze her hand, and she flashes a smile that melts my resistance. It's my family in there. My friends. My life she's trying to accommodate, so the least I can do is not be a dick.

Applause breaks out when we enter. Legit cheers and catcalls that seem several days premature in my opinion. *That's right people, we made it all the way from Suite 1401 to the banquet room!*

Callie is more generous with a shy wave, and I tuck her against me.

"'Sup, everyone," I call out, plastering my own welcoming grin on my face. Everyone's here, my brother Nate and his family, sister Molly, my other siblings, the rest of the wedding party. Hell, is that Uncle Nestor and his lady friend? Yep, dude doesn't even turn from the buffet to say hi.

Soon we're wrapped in a huddle of hugs, handshakes, and backslaps. Everyone wants to know if we're "ready for the big day," "having any second thoughts (har har)," or whether there will be an open bar at the reception. Kind of jealous of Uncle N who gets to enjoy his olive tapenade in peace. Judging by the obscene pile in front of him, he really, really intends to enjoy olive tapenade.

"Congrats, bro," Nate says, yanking me in for a hug.

"Thanks, man."

"You chose a good one."

"I know."

I glance over at Callie who's handling the knot of welcoming relatives like an all-star. They're my people, for the most part. Her estranged family wasn't on the guest list, although I'd love an opportunity to punch her dickhead father after the hell he's put us through over the last year. A story for another time. My blood's already heated.

"Where's Luke?" Molly asks, joining us.

"Of course you care more about him than me," I quip at my sister. She gives me a snarky look but throws her arms around me anyway.

"I'm so, so happy for you, Case," she says, squeezing me. "Callie is amazing."

"She is. Not sure why she agreed to marry me. Someone must have paid her off."

Molly snorts a laugh and shoves me. "Whatever. You're not such a bad catch either, big bro." She leans in again. "Did you see Uncle Nestor brought his girlfriend?"

"Hard to miss," I say. They're back at the buffet, even though their table is already covered with plates stacked with food.

"What are they doing?" Molly asks. As if I'm the expert on Uncle Nestor's psyche?

"No idea, but do me a favor? Can you keep an eye on him? You know how he can be."

She nods, not looking thrilled about the assignment. "I'll do my best. Hey. I've been meaning to ask." She bites her lip, and I do *not* like the direction of her gaze. "Is Eli still single?"

"No," I lie.

"Really? He's dating someone?"

"No."

"So he's not dating anyone?"

"Molly, I love you. My answer to inquiries about Eli will always be no."

Her attention starts to wander again, and I gently twist it back to me. "No."

She crosses her arms in the signature Barrett pout I'm pretty sure I've demonstrated at least five times since arriving at the hotel. "He's so fun though."

"Which makes him a hard no."

She has more protests queued up and ready, but Callie rescues me by slipping her arm around my elbow. "Hey, Molly!"

"Hi! It's so good to see you." My sister gives me a discreet glare to make it clear that's meant for only one of us. I smirk and leave the ladies to chat. I thought I saw Jesse come in and want to ask him about his new IEMs. I've been thinking about another pair for a while.

"Oh good! You're here."

How the hell does Rita manage to materialize out of nowhere like that? There was carpet, relatives, Nestor's feast, and bam. Wedding planner.

"Yep."

By her look, she considers this a huge, unexpected win.

"Did you know there are spiders in this hotel?" I ask because it seems necessary to re-balance the universe.

Horror spreads over her features. "Please tell me you're joking."

"Nope. Found one in our room. Don't worry, Callie made me rescue it."

"Rescue it?"

"Yep. I built it a little condo, gave it a back massage, you know, the usual spider-rescue stuff."

She arches a brow, clearly having no clue what to make of me. I don't feel badly. She should understand by now that we both live to rain misery on each other.

"I'll talk to management," she says, somewhere between serious and annoyed.

"Thanks. Do you know which menu items are the gluten free options?" I add, eyeing the buffet for effect. I glance back quickly to catch her reaction.

"You're not gluten free, are you? You're gluten free? No one told me! Oh my gosh, it's not a serious allergy is it?"

Okay, maybe that's enough punishment for now. I release the charm, including a smile that even works on Rita. "Nah, I'm just kidding. That garlic bread looks great."

She offers a stiff smile—a truce, I guess—but any victory for either of us gets interrupted by a wave of excitement. I don't have to see the door to know who just walked through it. Personally, it's a relief, because I'm hungry and could use a break from the show. We finally have an actual chance at food consumption now that Luke and Holland have shown up to steal the spotlight. Thank god your best friend is a superstar. I catch Callie's attention and nod toward the dinner spread while the crowd shifts their enthusiastic welcoming to Luke.

"Luke's here," she says dryly.

I smirk and grab a plate. "Yep."

"Should we rescue him?" Callie picks one up as well.

"From what? Being an iconic rock idol descended from the gods?"

"Don't be mean."

"I'm hungry. He's fine." As if sensing our conspiracy, Luke's exasperated gaze crosses to mine. His face is dressed with his patented stage smile, but I read the discomfort. *It's supposed to be your thing, dude,* his frown tells me. I raise a brow, saluting him with the Caesar salad tongs. If looks could kill… I snicker and toss some grilled chicken concoction on my plate.

"At least your family's accepted him back into the club," Callie says, still supervising from afar.

"I don't know. Bet he wishes they hated him right now."

"Wait, is your cousin asking him to sign her napkin?"

I bite my cheek to keep from laughing. Callie's already on the verge of being mad at me.

"Just enjoy your chicken, babe. Luke can handle Chrissy." Is the whole week going to be like this? Callie fretting over every one of our four hundred guests? Making sure *her* wedding is their fantasy? My jaw ticks at the thought, protective sparks steeling through my limbs. Not a chance. My family, my problem, and starting tomorrow, I'm confining my girl to the spa. I have no doubt Holland, Mila, Silvina, and Luke will support my executive decision. It's a fair plan. At the very least, sincere.

If only I'd known this would be my last night as a happily engaged man.

4: THURSDAY 8:23AM, 2 DAYS

"Casey! We have a problem."

We have a problem. Four words no self-respecting groom wants to hear days before his wedding. The glass door of the shower flies open, and I shiver at the blast of air. Or is it the look on my fiancée's face?

"Can you narrow it down for me, babe?" I ask, turning off the water.

Damn, it's stuffy in here. Hate hotel bathrooms—unless Callie's naked in one… hmm… I read her expression again. *Nope*

"Rita just called. The Rose Chateau is gone."

"When you say gone…"

Sexy hazel eyes bore into me as I reach through the mist for a towel.

"I mean gone. Burned to the ground. Charred rubble. Gone!"

It takes a lot to rattle Callie, but right now my girl is all kinds of frantic.

"So no princess ball is what you're saying? Does that get us out of the Welcoming bullshit at least?"

I push my knee between her thighs, forcing agonizing friction, and she slides closer with a soft moan. She's so damn irresistible.

"If you think you can charm your way out of this—"

I reach into her hair. Tilt her chin up so I can charm the hell out of pink lips. Her groan is all I need. She arches for more exposure, and I reach under that tight fabric. She tenses into my hand as I massage her nipple into a hard peak.

"We'll figure it out," I breathe against her neck.

"You always say that."

"And we always do, right?"

"I hate you," she mumbles while sliding her hands around my waist. They go lower until a demanding grip on my ass forces our hips together. More friction. More fire. So many reasons not to worry about shit outside of this room. I pull in a breath, hungry muscle rigid and charged. I'd rebuild that damn rose castle with my bare hands for her.

Seven days since our last real time together. My body screams for her. The fire becomes volcanic waves when her hands skim up my chest, pulling me closer, pressing, demanding relief.

"Casey," she gasps as I rock against her.

"Yeah?" I manage. Her fingers work their magic on me and—oh god. My own grip slides her tiny shorts down so I can enter her slowly.

"Ah... Case…" She arches again, moans that private melody I love. "I… ahh. We have to—"

I pump harder, ready to push us into oblivion. My eyes clench shut, air coming hard into my chest. She's writhing, so close. So damn close. Making me crazy. "What's up, babe?"

"Ahh!" She gasps out my favorite sound, jerks once, twice, a third, before curling over my body and wrapping her arms around my chest. We rest against each other in silence, one of my favorite moments. When our heartbeats and breaths slow in sync to form a perfect duet.

"You're amazing," she whispers. "I love you so much."

My heart. Can't believe I get an entire lifetime of this. "I love you too, babe. Now what were you trying to tell me?"

She sighs. Bites her lip, touches my cheek. "Sweetie, we need to call off the wedding."

"Wait, what?"

"We can't get married without a venue."

Callie pushes at my shoulders, gaze heavy with satisfied lust and broken dreams.

I don't move.

"Like Hell the wedding's off. We're getting married, Cal."

"But the Rose Chateau—"

"What do fucking roses have to do with anything?"

Her nose scrunches. "Language."

"You're breaking up with me. I think I get a pass on word choice."

She rolls her eyes along with another shove against my shoulders. "Don't be so dramatic. You know what I mean."

I straighten and cross my arms. "Do I? I can't believe a Grammy-winning rock star is getting stood up at the altar."

"The *altar* is a pile of ash, genius."

She shrieks as I nuzzle her neck with my two-day scruff. "You're going to leave marks!"

"What do you care? You're just gonna pout in the room all weekend."

"Jerk." Why does this woman love to hit me so much?

Her body relaxes into the sheets, and I finally push off her to my back.

"Seriously, Case. What are we going to do?"

I take her hand and follow her gaze to the ceiling. "First, put clothes on. Second, the Welcoming Thing. I'm freaking starving anyway. Then? We figure things out."

She squeezes my hand. Clings, really. "What if we can't?"

I twist my head over to connect with the most beautiful eyes I've ever seen. "Not an option. I'm taking my *wife* on this tour."

I leave Callie with the tiny lie that everything's fine. After all, Uncle Nestor is not a problem she needs on her conscience. Hell, Uncle Nestor shouldn't be on anyone's conscience.

Molly is waiting when the elevator dumps me on the sixth floor. Dressed in workout clothes with her hair tied up in a messy bun, it's clear this crisis wasn't on her schedule either. "I'm so sorry for bothering you, Case, but I didn't know what to do. You know how he gets and—"

"Don't be a buffoon!"

Molly shrinks behind me at the screech exploding from room 607.

An older woman with a grimace that matches my uncle's rushes into the hallway, hurling god-knows-what back into the room.

"You, two-timing piece of sludge!"

Ah. Cantaloupe. Why wouldn't you throw cantaloupe at your scorned beloved?

"They're crazy," Molly whispers behind me.

"What happened?"

"Not sure. I guess Uncle Nestor cheated on her?"

"Ya think?"

"They're going to end up with a felony if we don't calm them down."

I sigh and clench my jaw. "I'll take care of it."

"Thanks, big bro. Be careful."

I move toward the fray. Pretty sure I'll be down an uncle in about five minutes.

"Excuse me, ma'am?"

The woman's arm freezes mid-launch, and I'm relieved to see her melon arsenal is almost depleted. "Oh, Casey dear! It's good to see you again. Congratulations on your marriage."

"Thanks, Ms. Hawthorne. What's going on here?"

"*I'll* tell you what's going on," Uncle Nestor growls, shoving through the door in a leisure ensemble I can't un-see. "This witch is attacking me!"

"Oh god, Uncle N. Can you put some clothes on?" I block the view with my hand.

"I'll get dressed when I damn well choose. How about you tell this hag to stop throwing fruit at me?"

"Hag? Oh hag is it? You're a cad, Nestor Barrett. A bona fide cad!"

I draw in a deep breath. "Okay, look, I don't know what happened, but I need you to scale this back to a private affair."

"Affair," she huffs. "Appropriate choice of word. Wouldn't you say, Nestor?"

"Oh for god's sake, woman. I exchanged one dirty photo with her."

Nope. No, no, no. I glance back at Molly whose concern has faded into a traitorous snicker. She's loving this. That makes one of us.

"Your penis belongs to *me*!"

Oh my god.

"Hey." I step between them and practically push my uncle back into the room. His lady friend follows to finish the assault, and I give them each a hard look. "Here's the thing. You both need to start acting like adults because I have bigger shit on my plate at the moment."

Nestor crosses his arms. Ms. Hawthorne looks ready to cut off that penis she believes she owns.

"We'll need new table arrangements," she says. "As well as a new room. I will not spend another minute with this lying, cheating animal."

"Yeah? Well, maybe if you'd be willing to spice things up—"

"Stop." I clench my eyes shut and draw in a hiss of air. "Please, just... I can't." When I re-open my eyes, the warring couple finally seems settled into cool stares. "The hotel is booked solid for the wedding and some conference this weekend. As for the reception... I can't go there right now, so I need you to work this out or leave. Got it?"

Ms. Hawthorne sighs, and even Uncle Nestor keeps his grumbling to a dull murmur as I stalk to the door.

"Oh, and no more fruit-throwing." I call back.

∞∞∞

Callie is chatting with Holland when I return to the dining hall. They've become close, *besties* as she calls it, which definitely makes things easier for Luke and me. Right now though? I hate anyone who's blocking her from me.

"Morning, Holland. Can I borrow Callie for a sec?"

"Of course. So sorry about the Rose Chateau."

"Yeah, it sucks." I raise my brow at Callie and nod toward the exit. "I need you."

Her expression fades into concern, and maybe I kind of feel bad for the false alarm. Then again, what's the definition of emergency? Tension is already releasing from my shoulders at the thought of kissing her. Of absorbing her warmth, her peace. She can't be my wife soon enough.

"What's wrong, hun?"

"Everything that's not you and me in a hotel room right now."

Her cheeks flush. "Case..."

A grin spreads over my lips. "Cal…"

She bites her lip to cut off her own smile. "You don't play fair." I know what my smile does to her. So I have no shame, big deal. Her arms slip around my waist.

Shit. My blood rages hot. "You're killing me," I groan against her ear. I'm sure she can feel how much I want her.

"Yeah? You're the one trying to seduce me in the dining room."

"Is it working?"

The look in her eyes says everything. Her hands tighten behind my back, dip into my jeans.

"Please, babe. You'd have mercy if you knew—"

"Oh good! You're both here."

Fuck. Rita is the devil. There's zero doubt in my mind.

Callie pulls back and straightens with enough politeness for both of us. Good thing because I'm pretty sure there's a reason Rita avoids my gaze as she shoves brochures at us. "Do you have a minute to sit and discuss another option?"

I take a step toward the exit. "Actually, we were just—"

Callie gives me a look, and I grunt.

"Of course," she says.

We gather at an empty table, and I study Callie's face as she scans the brochures.

"I found the perfect venue. It's within distance range of the Rose Chateau and can accommodate an event of this size. It's a miracle they have availability, though I suspect your name has something to do with that." *My name* is probably the only thing she likes about me, and she seems damn proud that she got to trade it for some brochures. I'm not as confident as she is when I absorb Callie's reaction to the extravagant photos.

Her brows knit, jaw tight as she examines the images. "It's beautiful, but…" I know that softening in her voice. She doesn't want to break Rita's heart.

Not a problem for this guy. "It's kind of over-the-top, don't you think? Is that wall gold-plated?"

Rita draws back like I've slapped her. "They hosted a royal reception in the Champagne Room two years ago."

"Ah. Well then." I cross my arms with a grave nod. "Can they do a bacon fountain?"

I flinch at the foot that collides with my shin. It was worth it to watch Callie's shoulders relax along with her suppressed grin.

"*A bacon fountain?*" Yep, there's three words Rita clearly never wanted to say in sequence.

"He's kidding," Callie draws out. A quick warning look for me, and she focuses on Rita. "Seriously, thank you for finding this, but I just can't see myself getting married there. It's too much."

"What if we did a barn wedding?" I ask.

Ouch. Should've worn shin guards.

The humor in Callie's eyes doesn't match the stern look on her face. "Still kidding," she mutters.

"Look, can't we just have it here? This place is huge. They must have a bigger banquet room or something," I say.

Rita's expression pinches into a sophisticated version of *duh.* "Well of course my first conversation was with the hotel manager. Unfortunately, because of the large conference this weekend, they don't have a room to accommodate an event of this size. The most they can do is two hundred."

"Perfect. Let's start cutting," I say, clapping my hands together.

Callie smacks me, Rita looks ready to cry, and I sigh.

"Thanks for trying though," I manage. "This has to be stressful for you."

Score one for compassion when Callie squeezes my thigh.

Rita pushes back from the table and gathers her brochures with all the dignity of an *A-list* Wedding Planner. "I'll keep looking," she mumbles on her retreat.

Callie's hand climbs higher up my leg, and I hiss in a breath. "You're an asshole, you know that?" Her gaze has a different message and shoots all kinds of suggestions through my blood.

I grin and lean in. "Language, babe."

6: THURSDAY 12:29PM, 2 DAYS

Three words ruin my hope for an after-brunch encore of this morning's sexy-time: Wedding Team Meeting.

"Dude," I groan to Eli when he saunters into the conference room carrying a plate of bacon.

"What? They were clearing the buffet. Couldn't let it go to waste." He deposits his bounty on the table with a release so delicate I can strangely imagine the bacon cornucopia as a bouquet of flowers. He flops into a rolling leather chair. "Want some?" He pushes the plate two inches closer to the center of the table. Only Sweeny reaches in for a share of the offering.

"This stuff is the shit," Sweeny mumbles through a mouthful of food.

"Right?"

They shrink into their chairs at Callie's death stare. "You guys done?"

They nod.

"Good, so—"

"Sorry I'm late!"

All attention shifts to Derrick who bursts in and throws himself in the chair next to Eli.

"D, what're you doing?" Jesse asks his drummer.

"Wedding meeting, right?"

"For the wedding party."

Derrick grabs a fistful of bacon and drops back into his chair. "Yeah, and I'm the guest-book bitch." He bites through at least four pieces at once.

Jesse cringes. "Sorry," he says to Callie, who draws in a heavy inhale.

"It's fine. Just—"

"We should wait for Reece," Derrick says. "He's better at remembering this shit."

I watch Callie's sweet fingers clench into a fist.

"We don't need Reece," she forces out. Draws in a breath to continue—

"But he's Guest Book Bitch Number Two."

"Can you not call it that?" she snaps. My smile slips out. "It's attendant. Guest book *attendant,* and I can assure you we won't be covering any guest-book-related issues at this meeting."

Derrick holds up his hands in surrender, then reaches for more bacon.

"As I was saying," Callie continues. "We called you here to update you on some unfortunate developments and thought it would be easier to inform you as a group."

"Oh my god. You're breaking up!" Derrick cries, nearly choking on his bacon.

"What? No—"

"Damn, girl. Come here." Huge drummer arms that aren't mine, pull her in for a crushing hug. "We'll get through this," he says to me over her shoulder.

I can't even be mad that he's touching my girl. It's too funny watching Callie tense and look ready to smash him in the groin. She ducks away, eyes narrowed.

"Sit," she barks, pointing back at his chair. "I swear, Derrick Rivers, if you so much as open your mouth again, you're not only out of this meeting, but off guest-book duty."

Not sure which of those threats is more terrifying for the guy, but his wide eyes remain fixed on my bride as he lowers himself back to his chair. My fiancée is so fucking hot.

As she launches into the Rose Chateau Saga, I study the faces of our inner circle. Luke's expression mirrors mine. Amusement, concern, a glowing love for the woman barking out orders and updates. But the romantic side of his heart belongs to the lady to his left: Holland Drake, bridesmaid number two. Holland's typically compassionate eyes are narrowed into a threat against Limelight's drummer. Callie's newest BFF, Silvina, is next with her ever-hovering boyfriend-slash-former-mob-prince, Gioele, behind her. Something about that dude scares the shit out of me. Then my sister Molly, brother Nate, and of course Jesse, Mila, Eli, Sweeny—and Derrick.

My gaze rests on the empty seat beside Jesse for a little longer than the others. Parker's chair. It's been six months since his passing, and Jesse still leaves room for his brother's memory. Creepy? Maybe to those who don't get it, but for the rest of us, we can't imagine not including the guy in our lives. Those boys have a lot to be proud of, and Parker deserves to keep his place in our journey. My stomach clenches, and I force my attention back to Callie.

"So that's where we stand. We'll send updates when we have them so keep an eye out. Any questions?"

Derrick's hand shoots up, and Callie gives him a hard look. "What?"

"So there *is* or *isn't* a guestbook now?"

7: THURSDAY 1:46PM, 2 DAYS

"You sure you didn't want to check out the spa with the girls?" I ask Luke, while absently strumming my acoustic.

Luke shoots an eye-roll from the couch in my suite. "I'm good, thanks."

I smirk and stare back at my fingers moving over the strings. "What do you think of this progression for the chorus of 'While You Wait?'"

I play through the chords, studying his reaction as I hum the melody.

"Yeah, man. I like that." A smile lifts his features. "Run it again with the pre-chorus?"

I do, and his face lights up. "It's perfect. Sweeny can do a lead line over that. Here's what I'm thinking." He motions for the guitar, and I get up from the edge of the bed to pass it to him.

After playing with a few notes, he finger-picks a riff the guys will love.

"Dude, that's sick," I say. "Hang on." I pull out my phone and open the voice memo. "Play it again?"

Satisfied with the recording, I take my guitar back and return to my seat on the mattress. My hands find their natural resting place on the guitar strings and the light ambient soundtrack returns. Callie calls it Phantom Fingers, the fact that I can't be near a guitar without having it in my hands and strumming with zero conscious thought.

"Seriously, man. How you doing?" Luke asks.

I glance over at him and shrug. "Sucks, dude. You know Callie wanted to call the whole thing off?"

"What?"

"She likes things ordered. This is really hard on her."

"Yeah. What about on you?"

"You know how it is. If she's hurting I'm fucking hurting."

He nods, eyes connecting with mine in the bond that can only be forged by years of sharing pain.

"I just want it to be over, man. Make her my wife and move on with our lives."

"So why don't you?" I give him a look, and his lips twist up through the concern on his face. "She won't let you."

"Four hundred guests need their lobster and filet," I mutter.

"She's doing it for you. You get that right? Those four hundred guests are *your* friends and family. She has almost no one. She wants to make sure you have no regrets and the day she thinks you deserve."

I stare over in amusement. "She pay you to say that?"

"Maybe. Was it worth the five hundred bucks?"

"Five hundred? She got scammed."

He laughs and settles back against the couch. "Case, she loves you as insanely as you love her. I hate that this is happening, but we're going to figure it out. Hell, if I have to get that online licensing thing and do it myself right here, I will."

"So you'd wear a bridesmaid dress, tux, and a priest's collar all in the same wedding? This just keeps getting weirder."

"You think your wedding coordinator would approve?"

"Rita? Shit, she'd probably need counseling."

"Now there's a woman who could use a day at the spa."

"She wanted us to have it in the Champagne Room of the Bishop Crest Plaza."

"Wait, that giant castle where all the royals get hitched?"

"Yeah."

He snorts a laugh. "How'd Callie take that?"

"How do you think?"

"Damn. You'd look good holding a sword though."

"Wait, you think they include those swords with the wedding package?"

∞∞∞

There are two problems with the scene I find in the elevator on my way back to my room:

1. My sister Molly.

2. My bass player Eli.

"Where are you two kids headed?" I try for casual. Eli buys it because he has zero social awareness. I notice bikini straps peeking through a cover-up that could maybe pass as a dress on my sister. A quick glance at Eli's pants and… well that's no help. He's wearing jeans. My question remains.

"Molly wanted to go for a swim. Figured I'd be a gentleman and *escort her*." He adds a bow to that which has the opposite effect of chivalry.

"Right," I say. "In your jeans?"

He glances down as if noticing for the first time that he's not properly attired. With Eli, that's entirely possible. He shrugs. "I'll figure it out."

I shoot a glare at Molly who returns a plea. She has to know this is the oldest play in the book. No bathing suit equals a musician in his underwear, aka, kryptonite for nice girls like my sister. Not happening.

"That's nice of you, man, but I have some time. I can hang with you," I offer to Molly.

Damn. When'd she learn to wield those eye-darts? I swallow, backing up a step. And now we're at my floor, great.

"We're fine. Thanks, though. Enjoy your afternoon." Her words come with a shove through the elevator exit when the door opens.

"But—" The last thing I see is my sister's victorious wave.

I immediately head for the stairs, pulling out my phone as I walk. But who to contact with my SOS? Even Luke thinks Molly's crush on Eli is funny and harmless. Callie would help, but I can't add to her burden. Well, fuck. I put my phone back in my pocket and take the stairs two at a time toward the ground floor. That's where I learn this hotel has three water amenities, not including steam units and hot tubs throughout the resort.

Do I care enough to comb through every one? I try to imagine myself as Uncle Casey to Eli's children. Scratch that. I try to imagine Eli's children. Yep, it's worth it.

The first pool is a bust. This must be the pool where exasperated parents bring their exasperating spawn. I do find myself even more urgent to stop this Eli-Molly romance after that. The second pool is indoors, small, and reeks of chlorine. It's also packed with guests my uncles would appreciate. Wait...

I look closer. That is my uncle. I try to back away from the glass, but not before I'm spotted and beckoned with that wave only old people can do after years of practice. I draw in a deep breath, knowing I have no time to spare.

"Hey," I say, poking my head into the room.

"Well, Casey Boy. So nice of you to join us. We tried to say hello at dinner last night but you were clearly too busy for your Uncle Alan."

Passive-aggressive much? I see Uncle A hasn't mellowed since the last time I saw him at my father's funeral.

"Fancy a swim, young man?" a woman I don't recognize says. Her beckoning finger is frightening in its power. I find myself almost at the edge of the pool before I realize what's happening.

"Thanks, ma'am, but I'm actually looking for someone."

"I hope it's not your bride!" Uncle Alan laughs so hard at his own joke I swear he's the one causing those bubbles in the hot tub. Reason number seven not to get in. His companion joins in the laughter, though her eyes never stray from me. I can't help the feeling that she's hoping I'll end up in the water without a suit.

I clear my throat. "Okay, well it was good to see you. Enjoy your afternoon."

"Have you met my woman?" Uncle Alan interrupts with a strange hand wave toward Ms. Ogle Eyes. Is he drunk?

Probably. I search the deck for evidence of substances but only see the ginormous bottle of cranberry juice in his hand. Well… okay then. Hard to imagine why both of my uncles are single.

"Nice to meet you," I say, already backing toward the exit.

"Her name's Blanche. It's her stage name." He adds a wink as if that would do anything but lead to more questions I don't want to consider.

"Nice to meet you, *Blanche*." I find myself bowing. Damn those southern manners.

Blanche fans herself with all the charm of a woman who has a stage name like Blanche.

"Well, aren't you a honeysuckle."

I force a smile and nod.

"They used to call him that in school," Uncle Alan cackles. "Ain't that right, Casey Boy?"

"No. Not even ever." I take another step back. "Well look: again, it was great to meet you but—"

"Blanche here was nominated for a Pinwheel Award in the '70s, weren't you, dear?"

"Oh, Alan. You tease!" She swats him into another cackle, which leads to a cough, which leads to a giant swig of cranberry juice. "I was never," she assures me. "But it was certainly discussed at one point." This time her lashes bat with all kinds of innuendo I choose to miss. Plus, I don't know what any of that means.

"Okay, well, congratulations…" I think? "I'm sure we'll see you at the reception." This time I dart from the room before I fall victim to any more conversation. Funny that once I'm in the hall I find myself heading back to the elevators instead of the next public space. Molly's a grownup. She can take care of herself.

.

8: THURSDAY 3:12PM, 2 DAYS

I've just made it back to my room, found my bed, and closed my eyes for an attempt at a nap when a knock ends that fantasy. I press my fist against my forehead and wait. Nope, there it is again. Cursing, I throw back the sheet and swing my legs to the floor. I don't remember the path to the door being so long. I pull it open only to be greeted by a greenhouse explosion.

"Mr. Barrett?" the obscene bouquet asks. A face peeks around the side, and I sigh.

"Yeah."

"Delivery for you."

The man does his best to transfer his burden to me.

"Thanks," I say, grunting when the full weight of the arrangement transfers to my tired muscles. I stagger back a step, and the man smiles.

"If you can wait just a moment, Stuart will be here with the rest."

"The rest?"

"Yes, the cart."

"Hang on, what?" I follow his gaze to the squeak down the hall. No fucking way. "No."

"Excuse me, sir?"

"Those aren't coming in here."

"But sir—"

I place the flowers beside the door and pluck a card from the mass.

To the happy couple.
Marty Heilman

Who the hell is Marty Heilman?

"This has to be a mistake."

"You are Casey Barrett, Suite 1401?"

"Well, yes, but—"

He shows me the delivery slip.

"Are all of these from Marty Heilman?"

"I don't know, sir."

"Stuart" arrives with the cart, and I start picking through the bounty.

Best wishes.
Marty Heilman

Love is a gift.
Marty Heilman

Joined hands and hearts forever.
Marty Heilman

The fuck?

"Is this a joke?" I ask the poor man who shrinks back a step. "You know what? Doesn't matter. These aren't coming into my room."

"But sir, we must deliver them."

"Well, un-deliver them. Return to sender. Whatever."

"Sir?"

He and Stuart exchange a look, and I get it.

"Here." I return to my room and grab my wallet off the dresser. "A tip *not* to deliver these."

They look even more confused, but tentatively accept my gift, probably by force of habit. Their wide eyes watch me from immobile faces as I lift my hand in a courtesy wave and disappear behind the door.

I drop to my bed, pull up the sheet and have one of the best half-hour naps of my life.

∞∞∞

"Babe?"

A gentle tug of my hair pulls me back to consciousness. I blink and settle back to rest at the profile of my girl.

"Hey, Cal," I let out.

"Hi, hun. Sorry to wake you."

"It's okay. You can make it up to me." She squeals when I yank her down beside me.

"Casey!"

"What?" I growl, tasting her neck. Lavender. "I could have given you a massage."

"Oh yeah? How relaxing would that have been?"

"Who said anything about relaxing?"

I roll her to her back and push on top of her. She giggles and threads her hands in my hair to pull my head down. My body hardens and strains into the deep kiss. An intoxicating moan leaks from her as her legs wrap around me to draw me in. My eyes clench shut at the pressure of her hips, and—

"Sweetie, who's Marty Heilman?"

I freeze. Pull back. Watch hooded eyes clear and search mine.

"Oh, hell no."

"What's wrong?"

I push off her and rush to the door. Pull it open. And stand knee-deep in the English Tea Garden from hell.

"That's a lot of flowers," Callie says, tucking her arms around me. She kisses my shoulder and rests her head on my arm. So many flowers. Purple, blue, pink, yellow—an entire herd of unicorns vomited around the fourth-floor corridor.

"I told them I didn't want them in our room," I hiss.

Callie scans the mess of petals. "Well… They're not."

"Un-fucking-believable," I mutter, smacking my hand through the closest flower-vomit.

"Language." Callie rescues the arrangement from my angry fist and gently carries it inside. "It's pretty," she says, placing it on the desk. I watch her tend to the damaged buds and can't help but think what a great mother she'll make one day. *Thanks, Marty Heilman.*

"I'm really worried about Holland," she says, turning back to me. "She got sick and left our spa treatment halfway through. I hope she doesn't have a stomach bug." Her eyes widen. "What if we all get it?"

"Kind of fitting, don't you think?"

"Stop it."

"Hey, maybe we could have the wedding in a hospital."

She snaps a glare my way. "Not funny."

"A little?" There's that smile. I pull her into my arms. "Tell you what, you stay here and decide what you want to do with Marty's bounty while I go check on everyone and see what's up. Sound good?"

She bites her lip, glancing between me and the sad-looking flowers. How much of her brain is figuring out how to save those things from my wrath?

"Okay. Thank you. You sure?"

I nod. "Absolutely. You stay and relax."

"Casey?"

"Yeah?"

"I love you."

And there's my own smile. "Love you too, babe. We got this."

If only I believed it.

9: THURSDAY 4:02PM, 2 DAYS

I've just reached the lobby when I stop cold.

"Oh my goodness, Casey!" A woman shrieks and rushes toward me. Arms flailing and luggage falling around her, my mother is the picture of a war widow who just learned her beloved has returned after all.

"Ma! What are you doing here? I thought you weren't coming until Friday."

She throws her arms around me, squeezing any remaining protest from my lungs. "I came as soon I heard! I'm so sorry, honey. We'll get through this. I really liked her too."

"Who?"

"Callie."

I force her back to safer territory. "Yeah, I do too." Her expression is a little dramatic for a woman who just learned her son's wedding venue is a no-go. "Ma, what exactly did you hear?"

She swats a hand laden with costume jewelry across her eyes. Tears too? Damn. She's all in.

"I just never thought this would happen to one of my babies. Especially you."

I quirk a brow. "I mean, it sucks, but it's not the end of the world."

"Of course not! Oh sweetie, sugar, my dear baby boy."

I get dragged in for another rib-crusher. Yep, getting weirder.

I duck away again, gently holding her at arm's length. "We'll figure it out. Our wedding coordinator is working on it."

Her face shifts from devastation to disgust. "Don't you think that's a bit inappropriate?"

"No?" I ask, unsure since I've been confused by this entire process since the beginning. "That's what we pay her for."

"Counseling?"

Huh? "No," I draw out. "Wedding coordinating."

She freezes, eyes narrowing with vicious heat at a specter behind me.

"You have a lot of nerve, young lady," she rasps out.

I turn and capture the confused look of my bride.

"Hey, babe. Thought you were resting," I say, drawing her against me. Callie settles into my embrace and loops her arm around my waist.

"Yeah, I need a snack."

"You could've ordered room service."

She shrugs. "I wanted to try that café by the pool. I could use a cappuccino. Want to join me?"

My mom's jaw is on the floor when I turn back.

"You okay?" I ask the woman who's scrutinizing Callie like a bounty hunter. Callie returns a wary look.

"All right, what the hell, Mom? Why are you acting so weird? It's just a glitch. I told you, we'll figure it out."

"Just a glitch? Being stood up at the altar?" she cries, arms flailing again.

Callie and I both drop our hold at the same time.

"Wait, what?" I say.

"Norma told me everything! The wedding is off!"

I can't decide if the sudden rush through my blood is humor or anger. "Aunt Norma told you that?"

She nods.

"Ah fuck," I mutter, swiping my hand over my face.

"Why would she say that?" Callie asks, voice trembling.

"Because my aunt is a rumor whore and probably heard about the fire somehow which then morphed into heaven knows what." I glare back at my mother. "And you believed her? Come on, Ma."

"How many other people has she told?" Callie asks.

My glare transforms into a challenge. "Mom?"

Her chest blooms with color that flares into her cheeks. "So you're not breaking up?"

"Hell no," I say. "There was a fire at the venue so we have to find a new location. That's all." And yep, now I'm just annoyed. "Do me a favor and tell your sister to keep her damn mouth shut about shit she knows nothing about."

"Casey! Watch your tongue," Mom says.

I roll my eyes and sling my arm around Callie again. "We're going to grab some food. You hungry?"

I can't tell if she's relieved or disappointed at the lack of drama. That suitcase of jewelry was donned for a reason. My mother, ladies and gentlemen.

"I should probably find Norma to set the record straight," she says.

"That'd be great."

We watch her sulk toward the elevators, dragging her rolling bags behind her.

"Wait, is she upset we're still together?" Callie asks. "I thought she liked me."

"She does. But she likes making town headlines more." I leave it at that because I still want this girl to marry me. "Don't worry, I'm sure she'll have plenty more to get excited about before this weekend is over."

10: THURSDAY 4:28PM, 2 DAYS

Some foamy caffeinated contraption for Callie and a large black coffee for me. This is the life: my girl and I at a table, staring through a giant glass wall at palm trees and a sparkling pool. We're taking a freaking three-week honeymoon when the tour is over. Non-negotiable.

My phone buzzes, and I ignore it. Again. Ignore it. Again.

"You can check it, hun," Callie says, dipping into her parfait.

"No. I just want to enjoy watching you eat that yogurt."

She snorts a laugh. "You're so weird."

"Not my fault everything you do is so sexy. Ooh, can you eat the strawberry next?"

She grins and makes a grand display of sucking it clean before nibbling the end. *Shit.* I make a mental note to add strawberries to our next room service order.

Another buzz. Two more. Three.

"What the hell?" I mutter, finally looking at the phone. I just about choke on my coffee.

"What's wrong?" she asks.

"Crap." I shake my head. "One sec, babe." I return one of the many messages, and our manager answers on the first ring.

"Hey, Casey. I just heard. You okay?"

"Hey, TJ. No, actually I'm not."

"I can imagine. Listen, I'll start making calls to see if we can push the tour back and give you some time to recover, okay?"

"Don't. You can spend the time telling everyone to mind their own damn business and for the tenth time, Callie and I are *not* breaking up."

"Wait, what?"

"We're not breaking up!"

"But… damn. It's all over the place. Hell, you already have fan groups devoted to being your rebound girl."

"You're joking."

"I'm not, man."

"Shit." I scrub my forehead. Callie's lost interest in her snack, and I reach for her hand. "Okay, well, the wedding is still on. So you can start spreading *that* rumor."

"Wait, which rumor?"

"That I'm getting married."

"To Callie?"

"Of course to Callie. Who else?"

"Hey, no need to get pissy. I'm on your side, remember?"

I pull in a calming breath. "Okay, well, I'd appreciate it if you could set the record straight."

"Will do. The Label and promoters will be relieved."

"Shit, they're in on this too?"

"They're concerned."

"Fuck."

"Well, look. I'm sure you've got your hands full so give me a ring if you need anything."

He hangs up, and I'm about to fill Callie in when shouts draw our attention to the café counter.

"No way in hell I'm buying you more fruit!"

"I'm a grown woman, Nestor Barrett. You have no right to tell me what I can and cannot eat!"

"You're just going to throw it at me!"

Callie bites her lip when she sees my face. Nice of her to try not to laugh while I'm ready to pound my fist through a wall.

"That's it." I throw my napkin down and jump from the chair. She grabs my arm and squeezes.

"Babe, remember. They're guests. And family. Want me to talk to them?"

I sigh and shake my head. "I won't murder them. Promise."

The shrieking comes to an abrupt stop when they see me.

"Casey, good to see you again," Ms. Hawthorne says.

"Is there a problem?" I ask.

"No problem," Nestor mutters.

"Good, because if you two don't work this out in the next five minutes, you'll be working it out back home in your own house."

With a glare, Nestor finishes placing his order that now includes a fruit cup. Ms. Hawthorne crosses her arms in a triumphant huff. I return to Callie and drop to the chair.

"My hero," she teases.

I grunt and rake a hand through my hair. "I'm going to end up with a rap sheet if we don't find a solution to manage them. Guess I'll be spending the entire week babysitting two seventy-year-olds."

Her perfect lips rest on the edge of her mug as her mind works on something. Uh-oh. I don't know if I should be scared or relieved at her sudden smile.

"I have an idea," she says. "Can you give me Derrick's number?"

∞∞∞

My girl is brilliant. Derrick is thrilled at his *important* job of hanging out with Uncle Nestor for the rest of the week. So important that Callie said he didn't mention his duties as Guest Book Bitch once during their call. I love how she mouths bitch in barely a whisper. How did this saint end up with a heathen like me?

"Here he comes," she says when we spot him approaching the café.

I flag him down and accept a fist bump back slap.

"Where's the old dude?" he asks, scanning the tables.

"Call them Mr. Barrett and Ms. Hawthorne, okay?"

"No prob."

I have zero confidence that will happen as we make our way to their table. Ms. Hawthorne munches on her fruit cup with a look of ecstasy, while Nestor looks on with suspicion.

"Now what? We weren't fighting," he grumbles.

I force my irritation away. "I know. I just wanted to introduce you to a friend of mine. This is Derrick Rivers. He's here alone, and I was wondering if you two wouldn't mind keeping him company this week."

Derrick shoots me a not-so-subtle wink, and I return a tight smile.

"Oh, honey, of course you can pal around with us," Ms. Hawthorne says. She grabs his hand and yanks him to the seat next to her.

"Dude, I love your bowtie," he says to Nestor. Also, he means it. Wait, is that a smile on Uncle N's lips as he tugs at the yellow-striped flower explosion around his neck?

"Thank you, son. Mabel made it."

Ms. Hawthorne beams. "I did. I can make one for you too if you'd like."

Derrick's eyes nearly pop from his head. "No way! Are you serious?"

She squeals—squeals!—and grabs his hands. "I'd be honored. Let's go see if we can find material to work with in the gift shop. I brought my sewing kit. Oh, Nestor, do you mind?"

"Naw. I need more of my beefy snacks anyway."

I bite my lip, retreating slowly to remove myself from the weirdest exchange this hotel has ever seen. But hey, sometimes crazy plus crazy equals sane. Points for Callie for doing *that* math.

"They look like they're getting along," she says when I return to our table.

"They're perfect for each other. You're a genius. I love you."

She leans in for a kiss. "Say it again," she whispers.

"I love you."

I feel her smile against my lips. "No, the other part."

I chuckle, but my response catches in my throat. "No way," I hiss, looking past her. She turns to follow my gaze.

"Is that Molly and Eli?"

They're seated on a bench *sharing* a cup of ice cream. Two spoons. One bowl. Plenty of flirty glances and smiles.

"Are they dating?" Callie asks, surprised. At least she sounds more critical than pleased about that prospect.

"Not if I can help it. I'll be right back."

"Casey…" She grips my hand to stop me.

"Come on. Molly and Eli? Really?"

She looks from me, to the ice cream couple, back to me. "Yeah, you're right." She lets go of my arm, and I smirk.

"Be right back."

Molly's spoon stalls halfway to her mouth when I approach. Eli still hasn't grasped the precarious nature of messing with my sister.

"Hey, man," he says, swallowing a glob of chocolate.

"What's up?" I ask. Molly looks guilty. Eli shrugs.

"Eating ice cream," he says, through another mouthful. He cringes and presses his palms to his temples. "Brain freeze," he gasps out. After a moment, he shakes his head and releases a sigh. "Whew. That was rough. Want some?" He holds up the cup and his spoon.

"I'm good." This should be easier than I thought.

"We're just having a snack," Molly says.

"Right," I say, calm.

Eli shrugs and shovels another mound of chocolate into his mouth. I watch, wait, because… yep.

He hisses in a breath, presses his palms to his temples. "Brain freeze," he wheezes out again.

I nod, then glance at Molly who won't look at me. Apparently, she doesn't want to see my *Really? This guy?* expression.

"Well you kids have fun," I say, feeling like I've won this round.

Eli lifts a hand in salute through clear agony.

Molly still won't look at me.

∞∞∞

"What's wrong with Eli?" Callie asks when I return to our table. "He looks like he's in pain."

I cast a look back in time to see him trying to converse with Molly while he's doubled over. "Yeah. He doesn't know how to eat cold foods."

She makes a face, her attention moving to Molly. "She knows she can do way better, right?"

"She knows."

"So…?"

Molly's eyes have definitely narrowed into a glare at her date. Yep, that didn't take long.

I enjoy a sip of my now-cold coffee. "You need a refill?"

∞∞∞

I squeeze Callie's hand to the rhythm in my head as we walk. The air is warm, the sun bright and filtered by trees shading the nature trail running behind the resort. After the ambushes in the lobby and café, we decided to escape the chaos for some alone-time. Our phones are off, and ten minutes into our walk we haven't seen a single person we know. This is paradise.

"What song is that?" Callie asks.

"Which song?"

"The one in your head."

She holds up our linked hands as proof, and I grin. "It's the one I've been working on for the last couple of weeks."

"'While You Wait'?"

"No, a different one."

"It must be fast based on the pace of your squeezes." She lifts our hands again.

I smile and shake my head. "Actually, it's not. It's just in six-eight time."

"What's that?"

"Um… well, you know how songs have a certain number of beats per measure?"

"No."

"Well, they do. A lot of ours tend to be four-four, which is four beats per measure where a quarter note gets a beat. You know, one-two-three-four?"

"Like, the click thing with the ticking in your ear?"

I love that she tries so hard. "Well… no. And yes. Um, more like—"

"Did you hear that?" She jumps away, yanking her hand from mine. I turn as well, but don't see anything.

Hyperaware, her gaze darts from tree to tree.

"Spider?" I whisper. Not sure why I whisper, except it feels right. Man, I hope she doesn't make me find it and relocate it to another ecosystem.

She shakes her head. "No, bigger. Maybe a bear?"

"A bear." Is she serious?

Her finger rests on her lips. Then she touches her ears. *Listen*, she mouths.

Nothing at first. Just the birds and some environmentally appropriate ambient sounds. I shrug, and she waves me still again.

And then I hear it. A thud, rustling, the distinctive cry of a wounded animal. Maybe not a bear but certainly some creature in need of assistance. I start moving, but Callie grabs my arm, eyes wide.

"Don't go toward it," she hisses, clinging to me.

"Whatever it is needs help."

"How do you know? What if it's a bear?"

"Babe, there are no bears on the nature trail of the Florecita Hotel. Also, that's not the sound bears make."

"How do you know what sounds bears make?"

"I don't. I just know it can't be that."

"What if it's a bear pretending to make that sound to attract its prey?"

"So, like, a really crafty bear?"

"Super crafty."

I nod gravely. "That sounds like a bear I'd really like to see. Bet we could win some kind of zoology award if we document it properly."

"Shut up," she says, shoving me—in the direction of the rarely observed Houston Crafty Bear.

"I survived the killer spider. Bet I can handle this." I hold up my fists, prepared for a bear-throw-down. "Stay here."

My pulse picks up as I move along the trail. Not that I think it's a bear, but I'm also not excited about the rabid raccoon or squirrel or whatever is probably terrorizing these woods. It yelps again, close this time. Just around the bend, blocked by a tree. I press against it, peek around, and—

"Rita?"

"Casey! Oh my goodness, I'm so relieved."

I help her up from the ground. She brushes debris from her torn stockings, and I notice her lopsided stance. A black heel sticking out from the mud six feet back explains the first whimper. The second shoe, still on her foot and pressed into a patch of moss, explains this one. She slides her foot out of the shoe so she can stand level again.

"What are you doing out here?" I lower my voice, scanning the scene. "Is someone chasing you? Are you in danger?"

She bites her lip, trying to hide her emotion. Hard to do when your shoes are being held hostage by dirt and your clients have just mistaken you for a bear and/or rabid raccoon.

"I was looking for you and Callie. You weren't answering your phones."

"Yeah, we needed a break." I even say it without sarcasm.

"Rita?"

We both turn to see Callie. "Oh my gosh! Are you okay? What happened?"

"I had to find you. This couldn't wait. I have the best news!"

Any remaining darkness slips from her features, replaced by administrative poise. Admirable, sure, but it's hard to take her seriously barefoot and covered in forest crap. Still, I have to give her props for her effort on this one. She really upped her game (stiletto-jog through the woods?) so I do my best to keep a straight face.

She may look like a hot mess, but her binder is pristine. No doubt those cries were her sacrificing herself to save the folder.

"I just got off the phone with one of my large-venue contacts. She said if we can be flexible on timing we can get you into Houston Stadium!"

Her face. So thrilled. So sure we're about to burst into tears of gratitude.

Callie's, not so much.

I'm just trying not to laugh, because damn, she's actually serious.

"You want us to get married in a football stadium?"

"It's perfect! Now, we'd have to start the ceremony at seven because there's a concert later that day, but if we—"

"Seven in the morning?" I interrupt.

She nods. "Maybe it's a tad early, but if we combine some of the bridal party preparation items, I don't see why you'd have to be up before four."

I swallow. Callie looks pretty pale.

"Wow. That's um…" I don't really have a response for that.

"Think about it! We could even put your names on the giant screen!" There are actual stars in her eyes as she waves a hand in front of us to demonstrate the glory of our names. In a football stadium. At seven in the morning.

"Yeah, that's not really the intimate feel we were hoping for," I say.

"Well, yes. I know you said you preferred simple elegance, but I'm sure we can set up a trellis or two. Maybe a candelabra?"

"With all the stage framing, cases, and crates behind us?" I'm a musician. I know what a venue looks like before a concert.

"But there'd be plenty of room for your guests!"

"And twenty thousand others. Cal, didn't you say you were disappointed we had to limit the guest list?"

Rita's smile lifts and falls, lifts… and falls. She can't tell if I'm joking. Callie knows I am and glares over at me.

Rita clears her throat, clearly not liking the silence. "So that's a… maybe?"

Fine. If Callie won't, I will. "That's a no, Rita. Thank you for the effort, but if we wanted to get married in a stadium with stage crews and band equipment, we could do that any day in any city over the next three months while we're on tour. We were kind of looking forward to *not* being surrounded by random strangers and aluminum trusses for this one."

We wait in silence as Rita's face displays a range of negative human emotions—shock, disappointment, anger, despair—all through the filter of professional steel and flawless makeup. The result is a wedding planner that strangely resembles a malfunctioning robot. Just a glitch. Nothing… twitch… to worry… twitch… about.

I think it's funny as hell. Callie, maybe doesn't...

"Well then," Rita says finally, drawing all her dignity back into her shoeless five-foot-two frame. "I suppose I will see what other options are available." Distinct non-robot stress lines form around her lips as she turns and marches off, yanking her shoes from the mud on the way.

She stumbles a few times. Appears to step on some obstacles. Looks just generally miserable, and maybe I feel bad.

"Should I offer to carry her back?" I ask Callie, kind of serious.

"She'd probably stab you in the eye with her heel," she answers. Also serious.

"Oh did I just ruin your dream of walking down an AstroTurf aisle?" I tease.

Her eye-roll is a good sign. The smile that peeks through the set of her jaw, even better.

"I guess we could have gotten dressed in the locker room," she says, taking my hand again.

"No earlier than four in the morning."

We quiet for a moment, and then burst out laughing.

"I don't know," I muse as we start walking again. "It might be kind of nice to see my name in lights."

11: THURSDAY 6:31PM, 2 DAYS

I'm breathing through a set of reps on the bench press when my phone interrupts my rhythm. Eight minutes. Eight minutes of peace to blow off steam before I'm staring at the next crisis ruining my day. I'm not even sweating yet.

Rita: Found another option. Can we meet?

Screw that. I'm finishing my workout.

Sure, I type back to the group text that includes Callie. **I'm in the fitness room.**

I get a private message from Callie a second later. **Someone's cranky.**

Me: Yeah. And also horny, but I'm guessing she's not gonna help with that either.

Callie: Gross. Be down in a minute.

True to her word, Callie seems to make it down to me in just over sixty seconds. I'd like to think it's because she loves watching me work out, but really, it's probably more about her lack of trust for me alone with our wedding coordinator. Still, I strip off my shirt in slow motion as she approaches just to get that adorable eye-roll.

"Really? The universe already knows you're hot," she mutters.

"Yeah?" I take the bar again and push. Also, she's full of shit because her eyes are all over me. I smile to myself. God, I can't wait to torment this woman for the rest of our lives. She's not exactly innocent in those tiny denim shorts, and suddenly it's more than my muscles getting a workout. Pretty sure we need to cancel on Rita.

Too late, the third wheel's already bustling through the glass door with an armful of folders.

"Good you're both here."

I straighten on the bench so Callie can sit beside me. For the briefest moment, Rita's intense gaze fixes on my bare chest, and I can't stop the smirk at Callie's bonus eye-roll. She's dying to smack me, so of course I lean back and brace my hands around the edge of the bench to give "The Universe" a clear look.

Rita swallows hard, proving she's not a robot. Or an alien. Then again, aliens would have a vested interest in the human anatomy. I watch her eyes trying not to watch me and conclude she's human.

"I have fantastic news. Governor Brock Henry happens to be a huge Night Shifts Black fan and has offered his estate for your nuptials."

"The governor of Texas?" Callie asks.

Rita's head lifts in a smug tilt. "Yes! It's perfect. We can have the ceremony in the gardens and the reception—"

"You want us to get married at the governor's mansion?" I interject. "Is that even legal? Taxpayers and all that."

"Not the government mansion. His personal estate."

"How far is it?" Callie asks.

She clears her throat. "Only four hours."

The uncomfortable silence fills the gap in our response.

"We could… charter buses," Rita mumbles.

Callie's knee bounces, shaking the bench. I press my hand on her leg.

"I don't think that's going to work," I say.

Rita's chest inflates with a stuttering breath. Are those tears in her eyes? "I wish you'd at least consider it. Talk about it and—"

"We don't have to talk about it. I'm not asking our guests to spend another eight hours on a bus after traveling here."

"What if we find a hotel closer to the venue?"

"It's too much of an expense and a hassle. You'll have to find something else."

"What else, Mr. Barrett? What else!" Rita jumps to her feet, hand over her mouth. She looks about to speak before rushing from the room in a flurried click of heels.

Callie shifts away from me, and I turn to meet her glare.

"What? Am I wrong?" I ask, genuinely confused.

"No, but you didn't have to be a jerk about it."

"How was I being a jerk?"

"There are nicer ways to say no."

"Then maybe you should speak up for once."

"Are you serious right now?"

"I'm just saying, I thought you wanted me to play the bad guy. If that's not what you want—"

She jumps up and marches toward the door.

"Cal!" I call after her.

"I'm going to the room."

"Cal, come on, babe."

"Just go back to working out. Clearly that's more important than our wedding!"

Yep. And that's how I find myself alone again in the weight room.

∞∞∞∞

Stewing has never been a favorite pastime of mine. Who has time for that kind of drama? My fiancée apparently. One minute we're on the same team, and the next I'm the devil incarnate. I'll never understand chicks.

The door to the exercise room clicks, and I look over to see Jesse shoving his hotel key back into the pocket of his gym shorts.

"Hey, Casey. What's up?" he says, moving toward a neighboring machine.

"Hey," I puff out through another rep.

"You okay?" He studies me, and I'm sure my glare answers his question. "Anything I can help with?"

I shove the bar up again. "Just stupid shit with Callie."

"Wedding-related?"

"Isn't everything?" The bar crashes back to the supports. "I'm doing everything I can to deal with all this shit, and it's still not enough. She's biting my head off for every little thing."

"She's just stressed out, man."

"You don't think I am?"

"Yeah, but it's different for them, you know? No one expects much of us for these things. Our job is to show up and try not to make a dick of ourselves. For the bride, it's like some royal inauguration they have to host."

When did this kid get so smart?

"Yeah, well. She's the one who wanted all this shit. I would've been happy with a judge and a box of donuts."

He laughs. "Maybe, but I bet part of you gets it."

"I still don't know what the hell I did just now."

"Ha yeah. Does it matter, though?"

I narrow my eyes at the ceiling. Does it? "I'm just sick of this. If she doesn't like the way I'm handling things, then she can step up. I'm done. This whole thing has been a disaster since we arrived," I grunt, shoving the weight bar above my head again. And again. And again.

"You're going to strain your muscles, Case."

"Good."

Jesse shakes his head and loads more weight on his bar. "Look, I don't know much about relationships, and even less about what's going on between the two of you. But what I do know is that I'd give my right arm, my fucking *career*, just to argue with Parker one last time."

My chest tightens at the pain in his voice. I glance over and pull up from the bench. "Hey, man."

He looks away, jaw set. His fists clench the bar as if steel can absorb grief. "Anyway, my point is, you have to keep things in perspective, you know?"

Bright hazel eyes stare at me from somewhere in this hotel. Somewhere not with me and hurting and fucking *alive*. What if I never got to see them again? "I know, dude. I know."

A sad smile twists his lips. "Good." He drops to his bench and slides under the bar.

12: THURSDAY 7:03PM, 2 DAYS

I'm more annoyed than grateful for Jesse's counsel. Annoyed because he's a kid and inexperienced in serious relationships. Is Mila his first legit girlfriend? Probably. But worst of all, he's fucking right.

Our room is empty when I get back. Not surprised, I guess, and this pisses me off even more. She wants to run from conflict, fine. It's a huge resort. She could hide from me for the rest of our lives. At least that would solve our problems. Heh.

Still not sure what I did. Still not sure I care.

I rip the sweaty shirt over my head and kick off my shorts. Both end up in a pile on the floor that she'd hate. She likes things neat. Even dirty laundry should be discarded with Downton Abbey-like precision. I swear this girl lives as if the Queen of England could stop by at any moment. Why she agreed to marry my sloppy ass, I'll never understand.

Steam spreads over the glass of the shower door, and I step inside. Hot water streams over my shoulders, too hot probably, but it's what I need to tame the fire inside me. I cup my hands and splash the pool over my face, relaxing into the way it slides down my body. Funny how heat can cool. Another baptism from a hotel showerhead, and I'm feeling like a new man. Reborn into a dude who can't stand being naked alone. God, I love that woman. She drives me insane as much as I love her to insanity.

I turn the water off and maneuver through the bathroom to my phone. Pick it up. Punch her numbers like she's having the same naked epiphany in another corner of our private universe. Except Callie doesn't answer. Fuck.

"Hey, babe. Give me a call when you get this. I'm sorry." I toss the useless object back on the mattress and drop to the sheets. With an arm draped over my forehead, I wait.

I must drift off because I wake with a start a while later, still with no sign of my vanishing fiancée. I'm missing dinner, but who the hell cares? I try her again, then ring Luke when she doesn't answer.

"Hey, man. Dinner's almost up. Want me to hold it for you?" he asks.

"Nah. You seen Callie?"

"No. She's not here. Hang on, I'll ask Holland."

Luke and Holland exchange words that don't sound good for me. He confirms it when he returns to the line. "Sorry, dude. Holland hasn't seen her either."

"Shit."

"You lose your bride, Case?"

"Apparently. I fucked up, man."

"Wait, you? No way," he teases.

"Shut up, I'm serious."

"What'd you do?"

"I don't know. She didn't like the way I spoke to Rita, I guess."

"The wedding planner?"

"Yeah."

"What, does she want you to wear crowns and a scepter now or something?"

"Ha. Basically."

"Well, hey, if I see Callie I'll tell her to give you a buzz."

"Thanks." I massage my forehead. "Oh, and do me a favor. Don't tell anyone I lost the bride?"

Lost the bride. That's a thing, right? Pre-wedding jitters. Is she having second thoughts? I've never believed I was good enough for her. What if she's finally figured that out? Fuck.

I lean my elbows on my knees, shoving my hands into my hair. I don't even remember I'm still naked until a knock comes from the door. Slipping into a pair of boxers, I yank it open to meet a giant basket wrapped in cellophane.

"Mr. Barrett?" the basket says.

"That better not be from fucking Marty Heilman."

The basket clears its throat. "Sir, I—"

"Keep it."

"Sir?"

"I don't want it."

"But sir—"

I slam the door shut. Hmm… maybe this is what Callie's talking about? With a hard swallow, I open it again.

"Sorry," I say. "Thanks."

The porter shifts the burden to me, and his look of relief when his face appears makes me wish Callie were here to witness my munificence. I carry it inside, deciding it's tacky to take a picture of the moment, and grab a bill from the dresser instead.

"Thank you, sir."

I nod back and close the door with much less violence this time.

Marty's latest monstrosity stares back at me from the floor, every spare inch of hard surfaces already buried in flowers. I pick it up and nestle beside it on the bed. There's another card, great.

May the wind sing the song of your love for all of eternity.

Yours, Marty Heilman

I roll my eyes and drop the card on the floor.

The first thing that catches my eye is the cage. What kind of gift basket has a cage? I jump back at the flash of blue inside. What the hell? Ah, it's fake. So we received a giant gilded birdcage with two fake birds inside. Huh.

I reach in to remove the contraption and… shit! I hiss in a breath and yank my hand free.

"Dammit."

Blood puckers from scrapes on my knuckles. I shake off the sting and go back in to investigate—carefully this time. After removing the cage, I find the offender: a mess of twigs contorted into some kind of weird wreath. I guess it's supposed to look like a nest? More bird-themed crap rests below that, including a ceramic knick-knack my grandmother would love for her cabinet of useless dust collectors. I shake my head, a slow smile creeping over my lips. Well-played, Marty Heilman. You really outdid yourself on the crazy-scale with this one.

Stepping back, I survey the room with a mixture of awe and disgust. Grammy hasn't met a trinket she didn't want to display, and even she'd be horrified by this garish scene. Which gives me an idea.

I glance at the door, suddenly worried that Callie will return before I'm ready. This has to be perfect.

I yank the covers back up to the pillows and do my best to smooth the creases. With a fluff of the pillows and a pat down of a lump on the left side, I lean back to assess my work. Not bad for someone who lives on the road and never makes a bed.

Next... My shoulders sag as I scan the floral jungle surrounding me. Do I want a theme or just a random display? Hmm... chicks dig effort, so I need to go for it.

I begin tugging everything blue—Callie's favorite color— from the mass of decorations. Flowers, ornaments, those weird blue bird things in the cage—if it's blue, it ends up in a pile on the bed. Once I have an impressive stash, I start arranging them in (what I think) are attractive displays on the comforter and surrounding nightstands. I lay a path of blue to the bathroom where I spread more crap over all of the surfaces.

She's just stressed out, man.

Jesse's words come back to me as I stare at the Jacuzzi tub. Of course she is. While I've been focusing on rehearsals and our upcoming tour for the last few months, she's been bearing the load of this monumental event. She's never complained, never chided me for not giving more than a cursory okay when presented with her choices of what were probably infinite options. Weeks, months of painstaking planning to satisfy the expectations of a world she barely knows, and it all blows up in her face. Dammit, no wonder she's stressed.

I pick up the room phone and dial the front desk. I order a collection of luxury bath items. Then, I make reservations for two at the resort's high-end steakhouse for tomorrow. She probably needs a break from mass welcome meals with my relatives as much as I do. Hanging up, I step back to survey my handiwork. Not bad, if I say so myself, and it will be perfect once the bath supplies are delivered.

Now all I need is the bride.

13: THURSDAY 8:24PM, 2 DAYS

Who knew searching a gazillion square feet for a tiny brunette would be so difficult? No one's seen her, nor do they seem as concerned as I am. Then again, they don't have expensive bath crap waiting upstairs.

After crossing every crevice of the main floor off the list, I'm about to jump back in the elevator when commotion leaks from behind a set of giant columns. I join the steady flow of guests to check it out, my heart pounding because the odds are ridiculously against me on whatever this is.

What in the holy—

"Oh snap, there he is. Ladies and gentlemen, the groom himself, Casey Barrett!"

I stare over the sea of heads at Derrick who's set himself up on a platform with—is that Uncle Nestor's girlfriend? And what the hell are they wearing?

Applause breaks out as all eyes find me cowering in back. I fix a smile on my face along with a special glare for Derrick who's waving me toward whatever it is they're doing. A full drum kit, some hideous capes, and… is Ms. Hawthorne holding a flute?

"We were just about to perform, but I'm sure everyone would rather hear the iconic drummer from Night Shifts Black. Am I right?" he shouts to the crowd, which erupts in disproportionate excitement for whatever's about to go down.

I still don't know what the hell is happening as sticks are shoved in my hand and I'm being dragged to the five-piece kit.

"'My Funny Valentine,' sweetie," Ms. Hawthorne says to me as if I should know what that means.

"Huh?" I direct to Derrick.

"You didn't tell me your aunt is such an amazing flute player. It's been her dream to be on stage since she was a girl."

I swallow, my feet instinctively resting on the kick drum and high-hat pedals.

"She wants to play, Casey. She wants to shine. Let her be a star!" He's one high-pitched falsetto note away from spinning in circles with his hands in the air.

"Okay, but why does whatever this is require a drum kit?"

"Don't you see it?" he asks, waving toward my almost step-aunt.

I shake my head.

"Duh. It's a rock shawl. She made it just for this moment!"

"What the fuck is a rock shawl?"

Derrick glides to Ms. Hawthorne and leads her forward with the air of red-carpet royalty.

"Just give her a four count," he says.

"And then what?"

"That's it."

"You set up an entire kit to give her a four-count?"

"No, no. The kit is for the duet."

"The duet?"

"Yeah. She also plays that song from the iceberg movie."

"*Titanic*?"

"No. The one with the princess."

"What?"

"And the snow man with the— Never mind. Just give her a four-count for now."

Anything to finish this. "What's the tempo?"

He shrugs. "Depends what she's feeling."

"Why would I give her a four-count if I'm not actually setting the tempo?"

"Case, just relax, my man. You're doing great," he says, massaging my shoulders. I shrug him off and cast a look at the old woman who nods.

Tick, tick, tick, tick, I tap out and then sit back to witness the weirdest rendition of… well… pretty much anything I've ever seen. Ms. Hawthorne puffs away in her rock-cape while Derrick dances around behind her with the grace of a forest nymph on meth. Did they rehearse this? They must have the way they keep making eye-contact and nodding like this is choreographed. At one point, Derrick removes the cape-shawl from her shoulders and slings it around himself. More thumping and twirling—now with a cape—until the nightmare ends with an elaborate run of pitchy flute notes and awkward drummer pirouettes. The audience roars as the pair joins hands, bows, and then motions to me. I stare at them, frozen, and almost stumble over the snare drum when I try to stand at their insistence. The cheering becomes deafening when I manage an awkward wave for my part in this atrocity.

"Thank you, Florecita Hotel Lobby! Would you like to hear more?" Derrick cries over the roar. I scan the background for signs of hotel security, a pissed-off manager, anyone to put a stop to this. But nope, just a few porters and an assistant manager giggling amongst themselves. It would be just my luck that, for the first time in his life, Derrick Rivers had the foresight to secure permission before doing something epically stupid.

"Casey! Casey! Casey!" Derrick chants, while urging the crowd to join him. Soon dozens of strangers are calling for me to do something—god knows what.

"Play something, man," Derrick says.

"The iceberg song?"

"Nah, whatever you want?"

He knows we only have a drum kit, right?

"Um…"

"Do it! Do it! Do it!"

The audience follows the new chant as I breathe a quick apology to Callie. *Sorry, babe. I was trying to find you.*

I twirl the sticks in my hand, thinking. Maybe that's my problem: too much thought. This week has been nothing but cerebral exercises I'm grossly underqualified to handle. This, right here, however, I know.

Relaxing into the stool, I let instinct take over and explode into a rhythm straight off a stadium stage. Complex beats, dramatic fills, I lay it all out there for these witnesses, letting them know who I am and what music pounds through my blood. The toms, kick, snare, hi-hat, and ride, all become extensions of my body, extra limbs displaying my heartbeat for the audience. Once I start, though, it's always hard to stop. How do you halt the blood pumping through your veins?

By the time I finish, sweat drips down my temples, and even Derrick looks impressed. I flip the sticks toward him, and he takes them with a bow.

"Epic, dude," he says.

"Thanks." I draw in a relieved breath. "Can I go now?"

14: Friday 1:23am, 1 day

Crash.

Shuffle.

Casey?

My eyes flutter open and search the darkness. A shadow approaches, familiar when the scent of jasmine reaches my nose.

"Why are you on the couch, hun?"

"Callie? Oh my god." I shoot up and wrap her in my arms.

She chuckles against my chest. "What's this for?"

"Where were you? You scared the hell out of me."

"Oh, sorry. My phone died. I told you I need to upgrade soon. It barely holds a charge anymore. Can I turn on the lamp?"

"Please!"

With a click, light invades the room.

She gasps. "Oh my gosh. What happened in here?"

Her horrified gaze is fixed on my bed-art. Not good.

"It's for you?" I say-ask.

Her brow furrows. I guess confusion is better than horror.

"I wanted to surprise you with a relaxing night. I got bath shit too."

"Bath shit?"

"Yeah, uh, all those potions and crap you like. See?"

I lead her to the bathroom and flip on the light.

Fuck. Half the bath supplies have fallen into the tub. The other half is the packaging I forgot to throw away. The towel I laid out for her comfort is just draped awkwardly over the toilet, collecting who knows what. *Right. You nailed it, dude…*

"I'm sorry, Cal. For everything. I just wanted to—"

Soft arms slip around me from behind. Callie nestles close and settles against my back. I close my eyes, breathing in relief.

"I love you so much," she whispers.

Frozen, I pull her arms tighter, absorbing the moment. Is it possible to love a person too much? If so, that's my fate with this woman. I think back to the first time we met in that dive café. Luke practically forced me to go. Had to drag my ass out of bed because damn their little breakfast club was early. I agreed more from the spark in Luke that I hadn't seen in so long than the prospect of meeting some girl he thought I'd like. Looking back, I should have known right then that the woman who managed to reignite his will to live had to be special. "Special" doesn't even begin to describe my future wife.

"Rita quit."

Callie's announcement breaks that spell.

"What? When?" I turn to face her but don't let go. Never again, if I can help it. Last night was brutal.

"Right after we turned down the governor's mansion and she left the gym."

"Shit, Cal. I'm sorry. It's just—"

She reaches up to my cheek, her face igniting with humor. "Babe, we're not getting married at Governor Henry's house."

"Oh thank god."

"That's why I went out, though. Silvina and I were trying to find a solution and then got caught up talking at an all-night diner."

I can't help but smile at that. Of course she got lost in a diner, but I keep my comment to myself. She's on a mission.

"Any luck?"

"No," she says with a sigh. "I get why Rita was grasping for straws."

"Well, she should have told me too. Heck, *you* should have, Cal. I would have helped."

"Skeptical" is a good word for the look on her face. "She's afraid of you. I'm not surprised. Anyway, Silvina and I thought we'd be able to come up with something and we'd have a solution when I told you about Rita."

"I'm sorry Rita dumped this on you."

I would've expected more distress from my bride at the loss of our coordinator. Instead, she lets out a dry laugh. "It's okay. I don't think she ever really understood us or what we wanted. She had it in her head we needed some fairytale ball when all I wanted was a simple ceremony and dinner. I've been fighting her since day one on everything from the silverware design to the type of flowers for the centerpiece. Did you know you have to consider the level of interaction you want for your guests at the table when choosing the centerpiece height?"

There's a pinch in my gut, and I drop a kiss on her hair. We'd hired a coordinator to make the process easy, not to ruin it. "Really? Damn, my brain broke just thinking about that. Why didn't you tell me?"

"I didn't want you to worry. You had enough going on with getting ready for the tour, and writing and then Penchant had that—"

I cut her off with a kiss. Can't help it. Protect and cherish—so damn easy with Callie. "I'm giving you the best wedding you can imagine. I don't care what it takes," I say softly against her lips.

"My tastes are simple. I've only ever had one must on my list."

"Which is?"

"You."

15: Friday 8:23am, 1 day

She's stirring, which means fair game for me. I tuck my arm around Callie and align our bodies until she settles in with a groan that's not entirely of the annoyed variety.

"You're hard again?" she mumbles.

"Always for you," I say against her neck.

The groan is a moan this time when her hand reaches back and grips my hair. She pulls harder in tune with the climbing intensity until she tugs me over her.

"It must be hard being engaged to such a hot piece of ass," I murmur, shoving against her hips.

"You would know," she breathes out.

God, I love this woman.

"I'm sorry about… yesterday." My movements become rhythmic, eighth notes on the hi-hat to her effort on the snare.

"Me too," she gasps. Oh shit, I love the way she's responding with quarter notes.

"Keep that beat, babe," I say.

"What beat?"

"The quarter on the two and the four."

"What?"

"Just… no no, go back to the quarter."

"Case…"

"I'll meet you there in a second."

"Where?"

"On the two."

Her laugh breaks apart when I fulfill my promise. That cry is new. Also beautiful and the sexiest thing I've ever heard.

"Oh my gosh, Casey. What was that?" Her voice is little more than air through a sleepy smile.

I collapse beside her, wrecked and content as hell. "Babe, I think we found our song."

With a smile, she takes my hand and pulls it to her lips. "You see the world in music."

"And you're my muse." I toss a grin for extra cheese, and she shoves me with a laugh.

"Lame."

"You love it."

Her eyes rest on mine. "Maybe."

An alarm on her phone ruins the moment, and this time her groan *is* of the annoyed variety.

"I'm so tired. Can we skip the brunch today?" she says, throwing an arm over her face.

I move it enough to find her lips. "Absolutely."

She giggles and pushes me away. "I'm kidding. We have to greet our guests."

"Hmm, do we though?"

I get a legit swat for that. "Uh, yeah you do, rock star."

With a grunt, I roll away and check the time for myself. "Tell you what, how about I go and do the welcoming shit, and you stay here and rest."

Her expression softens into that sweetness I know so well. "Aww, thank you. That's so amazing of you, but Aunt Norma will be there today."

"Wait, really?"

"Yeah. No way I'm leaving you unsupervised in her presence."

Well, can't argue with that. That gossip-whore pissed off the wrong drummer. "Wait, how did you know she's coming today?"

Callie points to the giant binder on the floor. "Rita may be gone, but she left her wedding bible."

16: FRIDAY 9:47AM, 1 DAY

Oh hell no.

I see him first. Thank god, I see him first. With laser precision, I filter through crowds of lobby patrons to land on the bastard.

"Babe, I just remembered I have to take care of something. Meet you at brunch in a few?"

Concerned, Callie studies me. Fine—as long as she's not facing the line for check-in. What the fuck is he doing here?

"You okay?" she asks.

"Yeah. It'll just be a minute." I kiss her forehead, careful to shield her from his view. After escorting her to the hall that leads to the banquet room, I pull out my phone and send a message to Luke.

Me: Callie's on the way. Keep her at brunch no matter what.

Luke: Sure. What's going on?

Me: Her bastard of a father is here. I just saw him.

Luke: Fuck. Does she know?

Me: No, and it's staying that way.
Luke: Okay. Let me know if you need backup.
Me: Stay tuned.

Roger Roland was always on my shit-list but shot to the top after the stunt he pulled with the press last year to get his fifteen minutes at his daughter's expense. Should have known he'd show up for a reprise. Callie's barely recovered from the last betrayal; no way in hell we're doing this again. A voice in my head is screaming to let our security handle this, but damn if I'm not eager for some personal blood.

"Excuse me… thanks… yeah… coming through…"

Trust me, guy with the man-bun and lady with the dog-purse, you don't want to get in my way right now.

Roger's back is turned as I approach, and I have to suppress the urge to land a cheap shot. It would be so incredibly satisfying to see that man prone on the marbled tile. But that's not my style, and Callie would never forgive me.

Callie...

I manage to tap the shoulder I want to punch. Probably a good thing since my shower this morning reopened the bird's nest wounds. *Thanks for that, Marty Heilman.*

Roger turns, some trashy brunette I don't recognize hanging on his arm.

"Casey. Well hello—"

"What are you doing here?"

"What do you mean? Of course I wouldn't miss my only child's wedding."

The bastard has the nerve to smile. I clench my fist.

"You weren't invited."

"I assumed that was an oversight."

"You assumed wrong. You need to leave."

"Oh my gawd! I *love* your music," his girlfriend or whatever blurts out.

I blink, turning to her in disbelief. "Thanks." Back to Father of the Year. "You've hurt Callie enough. You're not ruining her—"

"Can you sign this? Oh my gawd, Roger! Casey Barrett is right here! Is Luke Craven here too?" she asks me. I stare at her, then down at the parking pass and hotel pen she's holding out to me.

"I'm serious. You need to leave before I call security," I spit back at Mr. Roland.

"And what would they do, Casey?" His calm voice only intensifies the malice in his eyes. Damn, I hate this man. "I'm a paying customer. You can't keep me from renting a room."

"With money you stole by exploiting your daughter. No fucking way, man. Get your ass out of my hotel."

My fist. Keeps climbing. Shaking. *Don't, Casey. Don't do it.*

"I don't believe it's your name on the deed to this establishment."

Is that a Rolex on his wrist? You have to be fucking kidding me.

"You don't know whose fucking name is on the deed to this *establishment*, so I suggest you get the hell out before shit gets ugly."

"So you won't sign this for me?" the woman cuts in, puffing her balloon-lips into a pout.

I turn on her, fired up. "No. I'm not signing your damn parking slip. You want a souvenir? Here's some free advice: Stay as far away from this parasite as possible."

"Hey! Don't you talk to my fiancée like that," Roger snaps.

"Oh funny listening to you pretend to respect women. Just not your own daughter, I guess."

"Excuse me, I love Callie—"

"Don't," I hiss through clenched teeth. "Just. Fucking. Don't."

My fist is downright trembling at my side. I feel the crack of fresh scabs from the tension. Good. A little extra blood on someone's face never hurt.

Flames burn in Roger's eyes as his smug look morphs into hostility. "You're not a father so you can't possibly know what a father feels for his child. The inseparable bond of—"

"No, but I know what an asshole sperm donor looks like."

"You can't keep me away from my daughter."

"Watch me."

"What are you gonna do, hot shot? Call your beef-head babysitters with the sunglasses?"

"Sure, not a problem." I pull out my phone. And shit, I'm not even sure *how* to call them. We're kind of off-course here. I could call Kenneth, or text Luke and tell him to send one of the guys at the brunch over or… fuck that.

I grab his arm and pull him from the line.

"Hey! Let go of me!"

"Shut up. We're done."

Loving the blood on his shirt sleeve. Just wish it was his.

"Hey! Security! Security!" The sack of piss shrieks like a child, free arm flailing, which ushers in a freeze around us. Dozens of eyes zero in and turn the lobby into a stage. God, I hate drama, and here I am, starring in the worst pro-wrestling match of all time. I let go of his arm and step back when three huge dudes from hotel security approach. Good, they can take care of this leech.

My co-star jumps away, his hand shielding the left side of his face. "He hit me! Oh my god, he hit me!"

"What's going on?" One of the men asks.

"This punk just punched me in the face!" Roarin' Roger lies.

"What? No fucking way. I didn't touch him," I spit back.

"Yes, he did. I saw it," the brunette says. "They were arguing and then he grabbed Roger and assaulted him."

"I did not!"

"Liar! Look at me." He pulls his hand away and... the fuck? Did that psychopath just punch himself in the face? Fuck!

One of the guards whistles. "Whoa. Hey, there." The others grab my arms.

"I didn't do that!"

"Right. He did that to himself?"

"Yes! I mean, I guess so?"

Roger moans in the Oscar performance of a lifetime.

"What's this?" A manager I recognize marches toward us, her gaze assessing the scene. "Mr. Barrett?"

I find the name badge pinned to her blazer. "Brenda, thank god. Tell your guys to let me go."

"You know him, Brenda?"

She continues to study us. "Of course. He's the groom for our VIP wedding. What happened?"

"This guy says he hit him."

Now, the idiot is hunched over like he just fell down a cliff. Fucking brilliant.

"Well, I didn't. Check your cameras. I know you have them. I didn't touch him."

"Actually, we saw you grab him."

"Well, yeah, but—"

"So you *did* touch him." The grips on my arms tighten.

"Only to make him leave!"

"And what right do you have to do that, *sir*?" The dude barks, all wannabe-cop-like. He looks familiar. Wait... is that the spider-incident guy? Uh-oh. "You think because you're some celebrity you get to push people around?"

"What? No, he's my fiancée's father—"

"Oh, even better. What would she think about this?"

"She doesn't even know he's here." Well that doesn't help. "Wait, I mean—"

The other guy's on his radio. Why is he on the radio?

"I think it's best you come with us, sir," he says, already walking me toward the elevator.

"What? No! I didn't do anything." I pull against them, which makes them tug harder. The third man closes in from behind.

"Brenda, can you take the victims to the office? We'll be back for their statements."

"Of course, Bill."

"Okay, you're making a mistake. I'm telling you. Look at the tape. Just look—"

"The best thing you can do right now is shut up and let us handle this," Super-Fake-Cop warns, and soon we're on a service elevator heading to "B." Nothing good ever happens on Floor B.

"Well, can I at least message my fiancée and tell her what happened?"

"This is an active investigation, sir. No, you may not."

"A what? You have to be joking. This is nuts."

"Do I look like I'm joking?"

No. He looks like he's overcompensating for something I have no interest in discussing.

At least the security office is as five-star as the rest of this place. We walk into a pristine nerve center of sci-fi activity. No flickering fluorescents or half-eaten salami sandwiches in this place, that's for sure.

"Okay, we'll need you to hand over any personal items, cell phone included," Bill says, waving at the device in my hand.

"Excuse me?" I say. "I'm not giving you my shit. You're not even a real cop."

Wrong answer, apparently.

"Son, we can do this the easy way or the hard way," he growls straight out of every Sixties western I've ever seen. This has already escalated to Crazyland, so I roll my eyes and hand over my phone. Pretty sure I can sue over this later.

"Wise choice. Sit tight while we call this in."

"Wait, what?"

Strong hands shove me down to a chair from behind. *Sergeant Bill* consults with the woman at the desk who's scanning a wall of screens. I strain for a peek but can only see what looks like a dumpster and auxiliary parking lot.

"This is crazy. I didn't even touch the guy!"

"Well you did, though," Bill sneers from behind the desk. I'm guessing the bravado is to impress the attractive female guard studying the security feeds. Too bad she looks as interested in a date as I am.

They're on the phone now, and I hear enough police jargon to know I'm in deep shit. *Assault, victim, suspect,* blah, blah, more ominous-sounding crap. Fantastic.

I let out an exasperated breath and rest my elbows on my knees. Burying my hands in my hair, I stare at the generic square pattern on the carpet.

"Excuse me, Mr. Barrett?"

I look up into the eager face of a junior security guard. Wide eyes, goofy smile, and no hint that he's about to explain why he's gaping at me.

"Yeah."

He blinks, still grinning.

"Do you need something?"

He shakes his head.

"Okay?"

He clears his throat.

"I play drums too."

"Yeah? Cool, man."

"I have a Pearl set."

"Sweet."

"Five pieces."

"Uh-huh."

"I can't play it though, because I live in an apartment."

"Gotcha."

"If I could I'd play your songs."

"Oh yeah?"

"Yeah. The grooves are sick. I'd add my own twist. Like, bah-bah-bah-bap and stuff." His arms fly with air sticks tapping out the imaginary beat. "I'd add more floor tom, too. I love the floor tom. It's my favorite."

"Huh. Okay."

"What about you?"

"What?"

"What's your favorite?"

"My favorite what?"

"Drum."

"Um..." I glance at the clock. Damn, the cops can't get here soon enough. Never thought I'd *want* to get arrested.

"Casey? Can I call you Casey?"

"Sure."

"You probably have awesome IEMs."

"I guess."

"Can I see them?"

"My in-ears?"

"Yeah!"

Seriously? "I mean, I don't have them on me, dude."

"Oh right, sure. Of course. Probably best if you're going to jail. Bet they'd get swiped real quick."

I stare at him in disbelief. "What's your name, kid?"

"Brent!"

"Brent. Tell you what, I'll sign anything you want if you go find me a bottle of Juniper brand sparkling water."

His eyes grow three sizes, and I worry for the safety of the head bobbing on his neck. "Juniper brand! Got it. Thank you, Mr. Barrett. I'm on it!"

He takes off, and I breathe a sigh of relief, praying there's no such thing as Juniper water.

It's at least another ten minutes before two legit-looking police officers push into the security office and assess the room. I'm a clear target as the only one not wearing a hotel uniform, but my buddy Bill leaves no doubt.

"Officer Andy, good to see you. This pretty boy is our perp. We prolly got a felonious assault with intent to use a weapon."

Intent to use a weapon? Is that a thing? By the look on Officer Andy's face, that would be a no.

"Okay thanks, Bill. We've got it from here. Will you come with me, please?" The officer says to me, nodding toward a conference room.

Gladly, I almost mutter out loud. At least this officer looks sane, and I follow him and his partner to the room. When I take a seat, I realize our threesome is bloated with one extra fake cop.

"This guy's a *musician.* You should probably check him for contraband, if you know what I mean," Bill says, motioning toward his "colleagues" with conspiratorial hand signals. Yeah, we all know what he means.

"Thanks," Officer Andy says. "We'll check it out."

"You know them celebrity-types. Always thinking the law don't apply to them. Good thing we nabbed him before he took off on his jet."

"Okay, well—"

"You laugh, but I seen it, Andy. Back in eighty-three when I just started this gig. I was just a kid outta school. Didn't know the games these perps like to play. Oh I seen things on this circuit. Hotels attract all kinds of riffraff. I remember this one time—"

Andy's fists clench at his side. "Got it, Bill. Hey, you mind grabbing us some coffee? You want anything?" he asks me.

I swallow. "No, thanks."

Bill looks less than pleased at being demoted from superhero to beverage caddie but the hierarchy he worships has spoken.

Once he's gone, Andy releases a sigh of relief that matches mine.

"He hurt you at all?" he asks me.

I shake my head. "Just took my phone."

"He what?" The man grunts and bobs his head to his partner. The younger officer gets up and follows Bill's path out of the room. "Sorry about that. He shouldn't have taken your property. We'll get it back."

"Thanks."

He takes the chair across from me. "So, you want to tell me what happened?"

"Nothing really. This is all bullshit."

He nods and pulls out a notepad. "Well, then you shouldn't have any issues. Tell me what happened."

I grunt and pull at the sleeves of my hoodie. "How far back you want me to go?"

"As far back as you think you need to."

I let out a dry laugh. "You know I'm supposed to be getting married tomorrow?"

"Yeah? Congratulations."

"Yeah. And every fucking thing has gone wrong so far. So okay, maybe I was less than civil when the asshole father of my fiancée showed up this morning to crash the wedding, but I didn't punch the guy."

"What *did* you do to him?"

"Nothing. I told him to leave. When he tried to bait me, I lost it and pulled him from the line and next thing I know security is on us doing some fake arrest bullshit."

"So you did grab the man at some point?"

"Sure, but I didn't touch him."

"Except to grab him."

"Well yeah, but I didn't hurt him or anything."

"No? So how do you explain the cuts on your right hand?"

I glance down. "Oh… Well, that… is… from a nest."

"A nest?"

"A bird's nest. Twigs and stuff." I don't know why I'm motioning as if that explains something.

He lifts a brow.

"Well, I mean it wasn't an actual nest, more of a wreath."

"You cut your hand on a bird's-nest wreath?"

"Yes."

"When?"

"Um." The adrenaline crashing through my system is seriously messing with my basic math skills. "Yesterday. I think? In my room."

"There was a bird's nest in your hotel room?"

"Not a real one of course."

"A fake one?"

"Yeah, it was a gift from Marty Heilman."

"Who's Marty Heilman?"

"Uh…" I chew the inside of my lip. "I don't actually know."

The officer lays down his pen, staring at me in silence like the lunatic I clearly am. "I want to help you, son, but I need you to help yourself by telling the truth."

"I am!"

"You're trying to explain away an altercation with a father-in-law you don't like by blaming your injuries on birds?"

"First of all, he's not my father-in-law—yet—and second of all, not birds. The bird was fake too."

"There was a fake bird at the scene as well?"

"Of course. In the cage."

"What cage?"

"The bird cage?"

"Which bird cage?"

"The one from Marty Heilman!"

"The person you don't know."

"Right."

After another pause, he sighs and shakes head. "Okay. I think we're done here. Please write it all down on this notepad while we go to interview the other subject."

"Check the security footage, there has to be footage, right?"

"We definitely will."

He stands, and I lean back, scrubbing a hand over my face.

"What about my phone?" I ask as he moves to the door.

"I don't think you should be worrying about that, son."

Fuck. Could this day get any worse?

17: Friday 10:58am, 1 day

I've been arrested before but never sober. And never for something I didn't do. Pissed isn't even the right word to describe my state as I stare out the back window of the patrol car, my hands secured behind me. Dejected, maybe. Frustrated, certainly. At least they had the decency to take me out a service exit of the hotel to keep this as low-key as possible. Then again, I'm sure Roger has already called every tabloid he knows to share the good news.

With the damning circumstantial evidence, the bimbo girlfriend's corroborating testimony, and my own admission of a physical altercation and hatred for the "victim," it's pretty clear I did it. My only hope was the security footage which turned out to be useless when it just showed a tussle in the midst of a crowd that ended with Roger in pain and me shouting at security.

Damn, maybe I did do it.

"You're the drummer for Night Shifts Black, right?" Andy's partner asks from the passenger seat. For the record, they hung onto my cellphone.

"Yeah."

"My kid's a huge fan. We were at your last show in Houston."

I work to swallow my irritation. "Cool. That was a good one."

"It was fantastic. Can't wait to see your tour with Limelight. They're a great band too."

"Yeah."

Funny how they suddenly have no questions about my identity. An hour ago, they made a huge deal about the fact that I didn't have ID on me. Well, yeah. Didn't think I needed it when I left my room for breakfast this morning. After convincing them to take me back to the suite to get it, I dug a further hole when I couldn't find my wallet. Still don't have a clue where that sucker is. Hell, it was probably stolen. Why wouldn't it be with the way everything is going? I tried to show them the bird's nest, but it only made me look more insane when I held up the handful of twigs I blamed for my mess. "We'll sort it out at the station" is a thing apparently, and now I get to experience it.

"Don't worry, man. We'll get you processed and back to your wedding as soon as possible."

What wedding? At this point we don't even have one.

Callie. Shit, she has no clue where I am. Last anyone knew I was about to confront Roger. Hopefully that one-phone-call thing is legit also.

"My fiancée doesn't know where I am. Will I get to call her?"

"Sure, once we get you processed," my officer-fan says.

"She'll need to find your ID and bring it down to the station as well," Andy adds.

"Seriously?" Fuck.

"Along with the bond money, unless you want to hang out with us for a while."

I shake my head and turn back to the window. I'd rather not, although with the way these past couple of days have been, maybe that would be better for everyone.

The car pulls into a secure garage, and Andy's partner helps me out of the back. Inside we get intimate with a security wand and a thorough pat-down. Again, not fun when you're not wasted, but the guys are professional and chain me to the bench to wait when they're satisfied I'm clean. So far so good, and I lean my head against the wall. The cool surface soothes the heat radiating through my blood, my fingers tapping out phantom rhythms on my legs. Arrested at my own wedding… Would Callie be more or less upset if I had missed the ceremony because I was in jail? As it stands, she'll probably leave my ass here to rot after everything I've put her through.

It seems like hours before Andy finally returns to collect personal info. After taking down my address, social security number, and other fun facts, we get to play the fingerprint game. Kinda wish we still had the drama of the ink pad, but the computer gets the job done, and soon we're ready for the photo shoot. Cameras I know, though they're less fun when it's a jail cell waiting on the other side. I line my shoes up with the foot outlines on the floor and flash my best mugshot pose. They also photograph the injuries on my hand—still not buying my fake-bird defense, I guess. What's that about the truth being stranger than fiction?

"You have any tattoos?" Andy asks. His hint of amusement tells me he knows the answer.

"A few."

"Arms? Chest? Back?"

"All of the above."

"Okay. Remove your shirt, please?"

I sigh and pull off my hoodie.

"T-shirt too."

"Do we have to?"

"Yep." A flash of impatience crosses his face. "We looked you up, Casey. This isn't our first date. Come on, you know the drill."

Yeah. But again, I didn't do anything this time. I pull off my shirt and try to keep my temper in check as they photograph and document all of my ink. Not an easy task, for sure, and maybe I start to have sympathy after a while.

"Who's Elena?" he asks, while examining the rose and dove on my left shoulder. "Your fiancée?"

"My sister."

He nods. "Sorry, man."

"Thanks."

He hands my shirt back, and I pull it over my head.

"Okay, this way, please," he says once I'm dressed. He leads me to a cell, and yep. We're really doing this. Another man is already waiting inside, clearly hammered. "You can use that phone on the wall to call your girl. Tell her to find your ID and bring money for the bond. Your conversation will be recorded."

The thought of asking Callie to bail me out—literally— the day before our wedding? I shudder. "Actually, if it's okay, I'd like to call someone else."

"Whoever you want. Just give the operator the number. You need your phone back to look it up?"

"No, I got it, thanks." A relief, actually, because, man, I don't need to see any flashes of the messages waiting for me on that thing right now.

"Sounds good. We'll come get you when it's time."

"Thanks."

The door closes behind me, and I feel a weight crash down that I haven't felt in a long time. Not since Elena. Certainly not since Callie brought her light into my life.

"Hey, son. No need to look so glum. I won't bite. Hard," the other prisoner cackles. At least he's not an angry drunk. Small miracles.

I pick up the phone and give the operator Luke's number, my pulse racing as she calls him collect. He's done enough time on this end of the line to know what my call means.

The connection clicks live, and I pull in a deep breath.

"Dude, a collect call from the Eighteenth Precinct? What the hell, Case?"

I swallow and lean my forehead against the wall. "I know, man. Shit is fucked up right now. It's a long story."

"Clearly. Callie is a mess. We're all worried."

My chest squeezes at the thought of her. "I know. I'm sorry. I'll explain later, just— I need your help. Can you go to my room and find my wallet? Make sure my ID is in there along with a hundred bucks for the bond, depending what it is."

"Sure, man," he says. "Of course. Where is it?"

"That's the thing. I don't know." Wait… Finally, a breath of fresh air. "My gym bag. It's in my gym bag. Next to the bed." My cellmate glances over at my enthusiasm, but he doesn't understand how badly I needed One. Freaking. Win.

"Okay, bro. I'll take care of it. But, Case…"

"Yeah?"

"I have to tell Callie what's going on."

I close my eyes, allowing the cold from the wall to seep into my skin. "I know. Tell her I love her, and I'm so sorry. And…"

"And what?"

She deserves better. "Nothing, man. Thanks."

"Of course, bro. I've got your back."

I hang up, sink to the floor, and wish I were as plastered as the dude smirking on the cot.

18: FRIDAY 12:43PM, 1 DAY

Time passes slowly when you're stuck in a box with a stranger. My fingertips are raw from drumming out the symphony in my head, and I've finished lyrics for three new songs. The worst part, though? Baldwin. The dude. Will not. Shut up.

"So then I told her if she wanted a vacuum so bad she should get a job as a vacuum salesman!" Funniest joke ever, from the way he roars. "Because, the discount, ya know?"

I rest my forehead on my arms, hoping that if I can't see him, he'll go away. At least get the hint that silence is golden, but this guy seems beyond the reach of hints.

"Who even vacuums ceiling fans, *amirite*? You turn those suckers on and let all the dust blow itself off. Self-cleaning. Brilliant little things. Dang, if I'd invented them I'd be on a beach sippin' umbrella drinks with one 'a them umbrella ladies."

I'm hazy on the plot from the part where the dog couldn't eat peanut butter because it gave him kidney stones. If there's any silver lining it's that this guy doesn't require active participation from his hostages.

"Dang, no. I'd buy an island. My own country, ya know? I'd call it... Country Island. There ain't one a those in the United Nations, right? Yeah, Country Island and we'd have free tacos for everyone. What about you?"

My brain stirs back to life at the pause, and I look up to meet a direct stare. What was the question?

"If you was rich, what would you do with the money?"

I shrug. "I don't know, man."

"C'mon. There must be something. All the money in the world, what are you doin' with it?"

I only see one thing. One face. One pair of hazel eyes I want to drown in and never breathe alone again.

"I'd get married."

He releases a low whistle and more cackles. "Dang, no way. Don't do it. I been there multiple times. Marriage'll kill you, amiright?"

Right now, death by marriage sounds pretty damn good.

"So what got you locked up?" he asks.

"Assault." I add a hard stare, hoping he gets the hint. Nope, it's beyond him.

"Yeah, gotta be careful these days. Used to be a man could use his fists like a man. Now you gotta be all 'please' and 'thank you' and 'my apologies.'"

More "modern" words come out of his mouth but I lose track again and stare back at the floor between my knees. My ass is starting to hurt from sitting on the floor, but I have no desire to move closer to my cellmate.

"Guess what I'm in for? Drunk driving. Can you believe it?"

"You don't say."

"I know! Used to be a man could unwind without the damn cops breathing down his neck…" Blah. Blah. Blah. Blah.

Kill me, please. Just. Kill. Me.

Activity at the door grabs my attention, and I force my stiff body to stand at the appearance of Officer Andy. "Barrett, you're up," he says, waving me out.

Thank god.

"What about me?" Baldwin whines.

"Not yet, Harold. You're still marinating."

"Fuckers. Used to be a man could get locked up…"

We don't hear the rest as we walk back to the booking area. Andy gives me my belongings, and I sign off that everything's there. After getting a ticket with my charge and a court date, I'm a free man. I totally feel like singing at this point in the process.

"Take care, man," Andy says. "Hope I only see you on a stage from now on."

I twist out a smile. "Oh, hey. You got a notepad or something?"

He lifts a brow and hands me one. I sign my name with a short message. "Give this to your partner for his kid?" I ask.

Surprised, he hesitates before taking it and placing it in his pocket. "Of course. Good luck, Casey."

He shoots out his hand, I shake it, and then lumber out to the lobby.

Luke is waiting, as promised—along with a petite brunette that comes charging at me. I catch her in my arms and bury my face in her hair.

"I'm sorry, babe. So sorry," I murmur.

She pulls tighter, nearly cutting off my circulation which is fine by me. "No, *I'm* sorry. It was my dad, wasn't it? Luke told me you saw him."

"We can talk about it later, okay?"

She pulls back and studies my face. "How are you? Did he hurt you?"

"I'm fine. Let's just get out of here."

Luke slaps my arm as I pass, and I pull him into a quick hug as well. "Thanks, man. For everything."

"I got you, Case."

"I know. I got you too, bro. Always."

19: FRIDAY 1:52PM, 1 DAY

Although desperate for a shower, it's food that occupies my brain's command center on the drive back to the hotel. We stop at a restaurant on the way, partly out of hunger but mostly because I'm not ready to expose myself to more drama at a hotel eatery.

Callie and Luke were quiet most of the ride, probably sensing my need to process what just went down. I'm a lot of things when we're seated at a table, but tired surpasses them all. Just. Plain. Tired.

Callie rests her hand on my thigh, and I reach for it like it's part of me.

"You want to talk about it?" she asks. It's so gentle, that look in her eyes as they search mine.

"I'm sorry, babe. As if you didn't have enough shit screwing things up."

She squeezes my hand. "Luke told me about Dad. I think I can guess what happened."

"I didn't actually hit him, I swear."

"I know."

"I wanted to," I mumble, picking up the menu when she lets go to grab her own.

"I know that too," she says through a smile.

Luke shakes his head, snickering. "Is that new ink, Case? You get it in the joint?"

"Shut up," I snap back, trying to hold my scowl. No luck, and we all lose it together. This whole thing? So ridiculous. Absurd, really. Sad, awful, and awfully hilarious.

"How's Holland?" Callie asks, when the humor settles. "Have you heard from her since we left?"

"What's wrong with Holland?" I ask, concerned. "Still that stomach bug?"

Luke nods. "Yeah. She tried to eat something at breakfast but couldn't keep it down."

"Damn. That sucks."

"I know. I had ginger ale and crackers sent to the room before we left."

Shit. Well at least she won't be missing a wedding... Maybe it wouldn't be so bad if we all spent the day praying to a toilet?

After placing our orders, I force the conversation that's been weighing on me for hours. "Cal, about your dad..."

"He's a jerk. I don't even know why he's here."

"Here? So he didn't leave?"

She bites her lip, and the anger that got me in trouble this morning returns. I'm about to respond when my phone buzzes. Mom. Great.

"You should answer that," Callie says. "She's been worried about you."

"Does she know?"

"About your brush with the law?" Luke is loving this.

"Yes, about my *brush with the law*."

"Everyone knows, dude."

"Really?"

Callie's expression is all I need. "Sorry, hun. He's right. It's all over the place."

"Fuck. So soon? How?"

Her teeth sink into her lip again. Yep, Dad-related.

"Well, he didn't waste any time," I mutter.

Callie points to my phone which is now ringing a second time. Fine…

"Hey, Ma."

"Casey! Oh my gosh! Thank heavens!"

"Ma, I'm fine."

"Are they treating you okay? Are they feeding you?"

"Who?"

"The prison guards!"

"Um… I'm on my phone."

"I know that, honey."

"So I'm not in—"

"I swear if they hurt one hair on your head!"

"I'm fine. I'm not even—"

"Tell me what I need to do! Who should I call? Oh! Cousin Al is a lawyer. I'm calling him. Just a moment."

"Wait, isn't Al in real estate?"

"Well yes, but he does real-estate law."

"Right, so…"

"Don't be smart. He knows other things."

"Mom."

"And I'll call Pastor Jim too. He's already at the hotel for the ceremony. Don't you worry about a thing, sweetie. We'll get you out in no time!"

"Mom. I'm not in jail. I'm at lunch with Callie and Luke."

Who are now grinning like idiots; my mom doesn't believe phones erase the need to shout from far distances.

"Out to lunch?"

"Yeah. I'm fine. Just hungry."

She quiets, and part of me suspects she's disappointed again. Norma probably had her all worked up and crusade-ready, and here I go ruining her plans. Then again, crushing dreams is par for the course at this point.

"Okay, well, be careful eating after so much time," she says finally. "I know how sensitive your bowels can be."

"Oh geez. Ma! I'll call you later."

I hang up, shaking my head as I tuck the phone back in my pocket.

Luke's hunched over, crying with laughter. Even Callie... "Hey, Case. The restroom's over there," he wheezes out.

20: FRIDAY 3:02PM, I DAY

I step out of the shower feeling like a new man. Funny how hot water and soap fix shit. Callie is on the bed, laptop open, pensive scowl on her face.

"What are you looking at?" I ask, running the towel over my head.

She grunts and scrunches her nose at the screen. "Trying to figure out what the heck we're going to do about tomorrow. Should we contact everyone and tell them it's off?"

I slide on a pair of underwear and drop down next to her.

"Ten Great Wedding Locations in the Houston Area" stares back at us, and after two seconds I understand her scowl.

"I really don't know, Cal. Maybe we can find a park or something and tell everyone to meet there?"

Her look tells me my idea isn't helpful in any way. "It's supposed to rain tomorrow. Plus, where would everyone sit? Plus, four hundred people in a public park? Oh, and permits because—"

"Okay! Geez. No park."

She sighs. "Sorry. You're just trying to help." Her voice wavers, and I glance over just in time to see tears fill her eyes.

"Aww, babe…" I pull her against my chest and let her sadness soak into my skin.

"I just want to marry you," she whispers. "Why can't I just marry you?"

My heart. God, is her pain going to crush me like this our entire lives? "I'm marrying you tomorrow, Cal. I don't care what it takes."

She looks up, tear-stained hazel pleading with me. "Promise?"

"I promise you." I still her trembling lips with a soft kiss. But it's not enough. No, words and kisses can only go so far, and this moment needs more than a promise. Callie needs the only thing I've ever kept from her: the secret I've saved since the day we met. I was too embarrassed to share it so early in our relationship, too vain to do it later when it no longer made sense. Now though? Now she needs all of me. Every shred of my love that has been hers since she saw me as just Luke's obnoxious friend. She has my soul; she needs to know for how long.

"Stay here," I say.

"Okay?" The suspicion peeking through the sadness makes me smile.

"I have something for you."

"A gift?"

"Kind of. A song."

I search through Marty Heilman's forest for my guitar case. I must look ridiculous fishing through a flower explosion in my underwear, but Callie waits patiently as I find my case, pull out my guitar, and start tuning.

"You wrote me a song?"

I nod.

"Aww really? When?"

I draw in a deep breath. "A year and a half ago."

Her eyes widen, brows knitting as she does the math. "Wait, we just started dating a year and a half ago."

"Yeah."

"You wrote me a song right after we started dating?"

"No. After the time with Luke in that café."

"The day we met?"

I nod, swallowing.

Her jaw drops, the tears returning, and I have to look away to hold my composure. "I've loved you for a long, long time Callie Roland."

And before she can respond, I start to play.

I can only dream of ending all the waiting
Praying that I'll see you again
Traveling the world, I've seen so many others
But I can't keep from thinking of you

But I still walk alone
Should I just move along

Since I'm far away, do you look for someone closer
Maybe one to sweep you away
Someone who can hold you
Like I've always wanted to
Oh how I wish that I was there

But I still walk alone

Should I just move along
Only time will tell
If I can be the one inside your dreams
Can it be me?

I don't mean to scare you
I just need to hear you
Tell me that there's nothing for me to fear

But I still walk alone
Should I just move along
Only time will tell
If I can be the one inside your dreams
Can it be me?

I have so many questions
That need to stay unanswered
How will I know the time is right

But I still walk alone
Should I just move along
Only time will tell
If I can be the one inside your dreams
Can it be me?

I hate to have suspicions
It's hard when there's a distance
Like the one that's keeping us apart
So if you feel the same way
Come on out and tell me
I would love to only wait for you.

I don't look at her the entire time I'm singing. I can't. Not with my heart exposed and pleading for her to understand who she is and how much she means to me. My voice betrays my confidence, forcing an extra rasp that's only there when I sing for her.

I strum the final chord and lower my guitar. Pulse pounding, head rushing, I clench my fist on its neck, waiting in agony as she takes in my confession. *Can it be me?* echoes between us. *Can it, Cal?*

Her eyes...

Giant pools of hazel sparkle from across the bed, stunned. I swallow, waiting, maybe even shaking, and I have to let go of the guitar before I break it. Good thing too, so I can catch the petite brunette who comes flying at me.

I laugh as she crushes me against the headboard.

"Oh my gosh!" Sobs choke out the rest, and my own cheeks burn with tears. After several moments, she finally sniffs and wipes her eyes. Looking up, she smiles as I melt into those endless pools. "Casey, it's always been you. Always."

I squeeze my eyes shut, holding her, loving her, desperate to protect her from anything that could ever steal that smile away. "None of it matters, Cal. Just us," I whisper against her hair.

She presses her cheek into my chest, clinging to me. "Just us," she whispers back.

21: FRIDAY 7:14PM, 22 HOURS

I'd forgotten about the rehearsal dinner when I'd made plans to take Callie to the steakhouse tonight. Then again, for a day that featured a brawl, a prison cell, and two emotional breakdowns, maybe a no-show at a hotel restaurant isn't the end of the world. Kinda wish I'd bailed on this event instead, though, because it turns out a rehearsal dinner without a rehearsal is kind of a bust. Half the room is in full funeral-mode with the awkward severity of trying to be appropriately sympathetic. The other half contains Derrick, Eli, and Sweeny.

"Want me to remove them?" Luke asks, nodding toward the three-man utensil band currently inventing a new genre of sound the universe doesn't need. We've got a drummer on knives, a bass player on forks, and a guitarist singing into a serving spoon from the tray of manicotti. At least they didn't mess with the filet and crab cakes.

"Nah, they're the only ones having fun. Derrick's last fill on the candelabra was pretty impressive, actually."

"How's Callie?" Holland asks me.

"She's… resting. Didn't feel up to coming down. How are you? Callie says you've been sick."

She and Luke exchange a glance. "Feeling a little better, thanks."

"Good."

"Do you know what you're going to do about tomorrow yet?" Luke asks. Is he changing the subject?

"Not a clue," I say. "I'm pretty sure our wedding planner sent out a message to all the guests warning them not to go to the Rose Chateau, but I don't know what happened after that. We'll probably go to the courthouse or fly to Vegas or something." I pop a green bean in my mouth. "What?" I ask the table of stares boring into me.

"You're not flying Callie to Vegas," Holland says.

"Why not? It would be—"

"She's right. Not a chance, Case." And I thought Luke was my bro.

"I don't know what else we're supposed to do. I promised her I'd marry her tomorrow. I'm marrying her."

"I get that, man, but what about us?"

I shrug. "You can go with us."

Would Holland hit me? Never thought so until this moment. "Luke doesn't mean he and I," Holland says. "He means *us*." She waves around the room.

My chest tightens at the sight. Friends, family, all the people who mean anything to us are here. They've put their lives on hold to come and support us. They're still here despite the uncertainty of not knowing what tomorrow will bring. Right… Guess we can't just ditch them.

Luke pulls in a deep breath and leans forward. "Okay, tell you what. Let's meet tomorrow for breakfast. Say, ten? We can talk through it and figure something out."

Sounds fair. Still...

Massaging my temples, I'm just about to agree when the dining room crashes to a halt. Literally.

We all flinch at the eruption, turning toward the bang in time to see a table being stacked on another table. Horrified hotel staff appear too stunned to intervene. Now what?

"Here ye, here ye!" Derrick shouts from atop the giant tower. Nothing good ever starts with "Here ye."

Silence settles over the room. Fear maybe from anyone who knows Derrick Rivers.

"We were going to save this for the reception tomorrow but since it doesn't look like there will be a wedding," (*thanks, man*), "we'll do it now." He glances down to Eli and Sweeny, waving them up to the table.

"I'm not getting up there, dude," Sweeny says.

"Why not? It's the stage," Derrick whisper-shouts back.

"We'll break our necks. Plus what the hell do we need a stage for?"

"Come on. Don't be a wuss," Eli says, climbing up to join Derrick.

"I'm not, but this is stupid. We can do it down here."

"It's not the same," Derrick says. Eli agrees. Sweeny crosses his arms and stays put.

"Fine. Wait there," Eli mutters.

"I will," Sweeny replies.

We all wait, actually, as the odd triangle bickers over proper positioning for their announcement. Not sure what's happening right now, but I'm relieved Callie is safe and oblivious upstairs. I might also use the pause to cast a smug look at Molly who doesn't appear overly impressed with Eli's performance. Yep, this romance is fizzling out faster than Grandma Barrett's half-used bottles of ginger ale she stored on the cellar steps.

Not much time for gloating, however, when the stage drama changes tone at the appearance of two young women I don't recognize.

Derrick launches into his seal-clap in order to bring the already quiet and confused room to attention. "Ladies and gentlemen, please welcome Lindsey and Heather!"

Someone applauds hesitantly, then another person, and another. Finally, there's a respectable wave of appreciation, and the girls bow. I can't tell if they're embarrassed or thrilled at their role in whatever this is.

"Who the hell are Heather and Lindsey?" I whisper.

"Merch girls," Jesse says.

"Huh?"

"Yeah, they're running merch for the tour. They've worked with us for a while. They argue a lot but you'll like them. They're solid."

Interesting. "Okay, but why are they at my rehearsal dinner?"

"Not a clue, dude."

We're about to find out.

"Without further ado, it's my privilege to present 'The Story of Callie and Baby Casey.'"

Well fuck my life.

I'm literally peeking through my fingers as Derrick and Eli jump down from the two-story table, remove the top one, and transport it to the open space in the center of the room.

Three chairs are placed around it, along with basic place settings. I'm still not sure if this was pre-planned until they pull out white t-shirts with names scribbled on them in permanent marker. Apparently, Eli is "Luke," Heather plays Callie, and Derrick is me. The other chick is "Waitress." Fantastic.

Sweeny faces us and spreads his hands. "Scene One: Breakfast Club," he says before taking a dramatic bow and shuffling backwards off the set.

Fake Callie sits alone at the table, tapping her fingers and looking bored while she sips what's probably supposed to be tea from an empty coffee cup.

"I just love eating breakfast," she says. "I only wish I had a friend."

I glance over at Real Luke who's nearly crying trying to hold back his laughter. Great. I'll be getting zero support from him.

"Morning, Cal. I brought a friend today," Fake Luke says, entering the scene.

Fake Me waves and bows, then does some kind of jig before sitting next to Callie at one of the open chairs. Luke sits on the other side.

"Wow. Are you in a band?" Callie asks.

"I am!" Casey replies, pumping a fist in the air.

"Wow. You're so hot."

"Thanks. So are you."

"Want to live together in Luke's hotel suite for a couple of months?" Casey asks.

"With Luke too?"

"Of course!"

"Sure. That sounds totally normal and not at all creepy."

Callie jumps up from her chair and holds out her hands. Luke takes one and Casey takes the other before the trio skips—yes, *skips*—toward what I'm guessing is Scene Two. Yep, here comes Sweeny.

"Scene Two: Suite 403."

Wow they even got the room number correct. This actually took research. By now Luke is barely upright. Glad he's enjoying this so much. Wait… I glance at him through narrowed eyes. "Are you in on this?"

He shrugs, wiping a sleeve across his face. "I may have answered a few questions and filled in some gaps."

"I thought we were friends," I say.

"Shh," Holland hisses, waving me quiet. Great, even the mature one of the group is one hundred percent invested.

I force my attention back to the strangest biography of all time and see that the three of us are now sitting on a bench with a ukulele.

"Oh boy," Callie says. "I sure do like writing poetry. I just wish I knew some rock stars who could help me turn it into a hit song."

"Wait! We're rock stars!" Casey cries, clapping his hands in Derrick's unique seal-style.

"Really?"

"Yes!"

"Prove it!"

I almost choke on my water when Fake Casey pulls off his shirt.

"Ooh those abs," Callie moans. Derrick winks at the audience and adds some hip rolls.

"What the fuck is happening right now?" I hiss at Luke.

"No idea, dude," he gasps through a chuckle.

I shake my head, the slightest smile escaping me because come on.

Casey puts his Casey-shirt back on—thank god—and Eli-Luke starts strumming the chords for "Greetings from the Inside" on the ukulele. Callie jumps up and dances around as she directs him and Casey, shouting things like "more strings!" and "play the four! Play the four!" Pretty sure Real Callie has no clue how the Nashville number system works. Or chords in general. For his part, Fake Casey just bangs drumsticks on everything within arms' reach while laughing maniacally.

"Not accurate," I mumble to Luke. "I wrote the song on guitar and recorded the work tape on keys. Didn't even touch a kit until rehearsals."

Luke snickers. "Pretty sure I wasn't playing a ukulele either."

"Damn. So glad Cal isn't here to see herself dancing like that."

"That was so good, guys!" Fake Callie shouts when the weird song comes to an end.

"I'm going to go be elusive and mysterious," Fake Luke says, sporting some serious vampire vibes.

Okay that was funny.

He slinks out of view, while the other two watch him.

"Good. Now that we're alone, can I ask you something?" Casey says to Callie. He takes her hands and drops to one knee. "Wanna date? Like, for reals?"

"Duh!" Callie says, throwing herself into his arms.

They stand and bow as Sweeny rushes back onto the set.

"Scene Three: The Tour," he announces.

AN NSB WEDDING 152

More props get moved around in conjunction with some deliberate hand motions, which means... yeah, I'm not sure.

"I think it's a bus," Jesse whispers. "Hey look, that might be me."

Reece runs into the scene, obviously missing his cue. Sure enough, his t-shirt reads: "Jesse."

Here comes Lindsey as well with... I squint for a better look and snort a laugh. "Holland."

"Still think this is hilarious?" I say, reaching over to tap her arm.

"As long as she keeps her clothes on," Real Holland mumbles.

I'm putting the odds at 50-50 at this point.

Back to the drama because now there's a dance party going on in our "bus." I must have missed that on the tour.

"Oh Casey, I just love touring with you and sharing a bunk on the bus!"

We definitely didn't.

"Me too, babe."

It's nearly impossible to focus on the dialogue with Fake Luke and Fake Holland fake-making-out behind them.

"Dude, get a room," I toss over to Real Luke. He rolls his eyes and mumbles an apology to Real Holland.

"Oh Casey," Fake Callie cries, the back of her hand to her forehead.

"Yes, my darling?"

"I'm simply parched. Would you be a doll and go to catering to get all the tea, my love?"

"All the tea?"

"All of it."

"And all the pineapple for me!" Fake Holland calls out.

My snicker draws a glare from Holland. First part of this re-enactment that's actually pretty accurate.

"I didn't eat *all* the pineapple," she snaps.

"Maybe not, but Cal definitely drank all the tea."

Luke chuckles, and Holland turns her glare on him. "What? It's kinda true."

Back on stage, our tour is now... who the hell knows? There's a fake plant and two end tables in the mix.

Fake Jesse is "performing" in front of the plant. After a ridiculous bow, he addresses us. "Hi, I'm Jesse Everett. No one's ever heard of me at this point, but I'm God's gift to music. I make men cry and ladies melt with my vocal magic. I'm also a total masochist who shacked up with the woman who ruined my life."

Also true. Luke and I are both cracking up now, especially when Real Jesse shakes his head with a shy smirk. Mila whispers something to him, and he covers his face. I'm just glad we seem to have sidetracked from the Callie/Casey plotline. Oh, wait, nope, there we are again.

We stroll arm-in-arm between the end tables, inspecting each closely. I squint at the action, trying to figure out what the hell we're doing.

"Oh Casey!" And why does Callie start every sentence with "oh Casey"? "This one!"

She reaches for some invisible object and holds it up to the light.

"Are you sure, my sweet?" Casey looks around. "I sure hope no one notices that we're in a jewelry store. Then they'd know we like each other."

Ah. That.

I smirk and shake my head.

"Right. We can't have people thinking we're serious about each other," Callie says, pressing her palms to her cheeks.

"That would be terrible. The horror!" Fake Me replies.

"What would people say? Two consenting adults in a stable, loving relationship? We must keep this a secret!"

Okay, point taken. Can we move on?

Sweeny runs out as the others clear the set. "Scene Four: The Proposal."

Wait... that was private. I knew Cal wouldn't want a big public affair, so one night I got us a suite, decked it out with all her favorites, ordered her go-to movie, and when I got up to pour us some champagne, grabbed the ring. She cried. I may have teared up too, and then we finished the film. That's Cal and I. Always has been. Casual, stable, secure, we just *knew*. So how does this parody have a Proposal Scene?

Sweeny exits the stage and... nothing. I burst out laughing at the empty space, relieved our private moment is still private.

"You ever gonna tell us the story, Case?" Sweeny shouts over to me.

I grin and shake my head. "Not a chance, dude. Better just move on."

Scene Five consists mainly of Callie watching us do shit. Whether we're writing, rehearsing, or recording, Callie's always there, looking somewhat bored as portrayed by "Heather." This scene couldn't be further from the truth—my girl is a badass powerhouse of activity—but it's interesting to see how supportive the guys see her. She's a fixture in our circle, as she should be. Kinda makes me proud, not gonna lie.

Scene Six brings us full-circle to the hotel for the wedding. This should be interesting.

Lindsey is back as Rita, telling us a meteor crashed into the venue and destroyed it. There are also some theories about alien life and unsolved mysteries that have absolutely nothing to do with anything.

"Oh Casey! Whatever shall we do?" Callie cries, once they're alone.

"I don't know, baby, but I'm going to the gym. Good luck!"

Nice. I roll my eyes.

Oh, and now I'm getting arrested. Great. I glance over at Mom who is clearly not enjoying Scene Six. There's way more fighting and yelling involved in this version. Also, I don't recall ever crying out about the injustice of humanity or whatever. Hard to understand Casey's point through his desperate sobs and flailing. Finally, I'm in prison where Callie visits me. I also look more like an inmate on death row than some dude who's been locked up for an hour.

"Baby, I'll get you out, I swear it!" she says, all drama.

"No, my love. You must forget about me. There's no hope for us now," I say, turning away and holding up my hand.

Oh geez.

"Never! I could never love another man."

I turn back with wide eyes. "Really?"

"Even if we can't marry in the eyes of man, we shall always be one in the eyes of God."

I shake my head with a smirk. This script has Marty Heilman written all over it. Wait… I squint at my bandmates. No way… I'm definitely investigating that later.

After my release, Callie and I walk away hand-in-hand as Sweeny comes barreling back onstage.

"What will happen next?" He covers his mouth in what I'm assuming is supposed to be a portrayal of "mystery." Or he's about to puke. "To. Be. Determined."

Not a bad ending, I guess.

The rest of the troop joins him in a crooked line. They hold hands, and applause fills the room as they bow.

Luke leans toward me. "Wow. They must have spent at least twenty minutes planning that."

∞∞∞∞

The room is dark when I return around ten. My heart sinks at the movement on the bed, and I place the bag I'd brought on the dresser. Turning on the lamp, I meet large hazel eyes, shining with tears in the darkness.

"Hey, babe," I say gently, sitting on the mattress beside her. "I brought you some food in case you're hungry."

"I'm not."

"Move over."

She shifts toward the middle, and I slide in behind her, pulling her against me.

"I'm supposed to be crazy with excitement right now," she whispers, voice trembling. "You're supposed to be nervous and joking with the guys. Instead…"

I squeeze her tight, resting my lips against her hair. "I know, babe. I know."

"I shouldn't care. I know it's stupid but…" Her voice breaks into a rush of sobs, and my heart shatters. I can't handle her pain. These fucking problems I can't fix for her. I'd give anything—*anything*—to make this okay. There are so many things I could say right now. Lies to tell her, promises

I can't keep, but we're beyond that now. We're alone in the universe.

"Cal?"

She sniffs and burrows closer to me. "Yeah?"

"You're more than my world." I close my eyes, breathing in everything she is, everything I want with her. "You're my story now. For the rest of my life. Nothing will ever change that."

Her grip tightens on my arm, and maybe for a brief second I believe everything will work itself out.

"How was the dinner?" she asks, after a long pause.

I clear my throat. "Um... yeah."

22: SATURDAY 8:51 AM, 7 HOURS

I glare at my phone and drop it on the bed next to me with a groan.

"Who's that?" Callie asks, stretching beside me.

"Luke. Wants to make sure we're still on for breakfast in an hour."

"Ugh, really? Gross. Have fun."

I reach over and crush her from behind. "Uh, you're coming with me, princess."

"No thanks. I'll pass."

"You already skipped dinner; you're eating breakfast. Besides, we're going to discuss the wedding and try to figure something out."

"We didn't figure anything out with the help of a professional wedding planner. What are the three of us going to do a couple of hours before?"

"Not sure, babe, but at least it will involve food. Get your cute ass in the shower. I'm happy to help if you want."

I grunt when her elbow meets my side.

∞∞∞∞

Luke arrives at our suite just before ten. Callie is still finishing up what she calls "light makeup" because apparently that's what's required for breakfast. I've learned not to argue, even though I don't think she needs any of that shit. She looks hot as hell in her ripped jeans and fancy sweatshirt that shows plenty of elaborate bra strap thingies above the low-cut back. Since it was supposed to be our wedding day, I put on a button-down shirt with rolled up sleeves that I know she likes. Something about the way it accentuates my eyes, I don't know. I even swing her favorite jeans, which, for the record, quickly became my favorite when she couldn't keep her hands off my ass the last time I wore them. Hell, the least I can do is look good for her today.

"You coming, babe?" I call toward the bathroom.

"Almost done!"

Luke and I exchange a *don't rush them* look.

"Hey, Cal. I heard this place imports their breakfast teas directly from the UK," Luke says.

"Oh my gosh, really?" Callie snaps around the corner, eyes wide.

He grins when he sees her. God she's beautiful—I'm a freaking mess. Who needs a fucking wedding gown? And that smile?

I pull her against me and plant a kiss on her head. "I'm buying you all the tea in the world, babe," I say.

She wraps her arms around my waist and squeezes. "And I'll let you eat all the bacon you want without complaining."

Luke snickers. "Aww you wrote your own vows?"

"Shut up," I laugh.

Cal grabs her purse, and we follow Luke into the hallway. "Where's Holland? Still not feeling well?" Callie asks.

"Yeah. She's going to try to meet us later."

"She should really see a doctor. This doesn't sound good."

"She will."

I find it strange how close Luke hovers on the other side of Callie in the elevator. Even stranger when the display clicks toward the lobby and he takes her arm. "You go ahead, Case. I have to talk to Callie for a second."

She looks confused but shrugs as we step off. "We'll catch up with you," she says to me.

I leave them at the elevators to head toward the main area of the lobby. As I come around the corner my heart stops. I stop. Everything stops. My jaw falls open, limbs go numb. I've never fainted before but if there was ever a time…

Holland comes forward with a huge grin on her face. "Over here," she says, leading me toward a cocktail table covered with candles.

"What the…" I can't speak, can barely think as my gaze scans what has to be dozens, if not hundreds, of my friends and family packed into the hotel lobby. Flowers and candles decorate every crack that doesn't have a person, and I'm the most underdressed guest in the room. Pastor Jim emerges from behind a column and stands beside me. My groomsmen line up behind me as well.

All except Luke.

Who still has Callie by the elevators.

Oh my god.

Tears well in my eyes. I swat them away but they just refill. My heart pounds when I notice the path that opens up to the elevators. Music starts to play, and there she is, the most beautiful, perfect woman on the planet floating toward me on Luke's arm. He has to practically hold her up when the shock that just hit me slams into her. So much for that light makeup. It's now melting down her cheeks when her teary gaze rests on mine.

I'm shaking as they move up the aisle. Full-on trembling with each step that brings her closer to me. The music disappears. The decorations. The crowd. It's just Callie Roland. My dream girl. My story that I get to live every day for the rest of my life. What have I done to deserve this moment?

Her smile, her eyes, everything about her is too much when she and Luke finally reach me. He lets her go, and I don't give a damn about wedding protocol. She rushes into me at the same moment I pull her into my arms.

Finally, we manage to separate enough to focus on Pastor Jim who says a bunch of wedding stuff I can't absorb. I'm hoping someone's recording this for us, because right now all I can see is Callie. All I can hear are her small hiccups. All I can smell is the scent of her hair, and all I feel is the warmth of her skin. The rest seems irrelevant.

Honestly, I don't leave the cloud until Pastor Jim stops speaking and Callie's hiccups become a full-on gasp. I follow her gaze to the small platform off to the left, and there's Luke, guitar in hand, Holland at his side. They must have raided the hotel's AV equipment for this setup, because it's a respectable mix of mics and amps. Jesse's at a keyboard behind them, along with a string quartet. Holy shit.

"This is a song Callie wrote for you, Case," Luke says, winking at my bride. She covers her mouth, overcome. I stare down at her in shock and pretty much melt when she looks up, all the love in her eyes.

"We were going to surprise you with this," she whispers. "Luke and I have been working on it all summer."

Afraid to speak, I pull in a deep breath and nod, tucking her tightly against me.

Jesse starts to play, the strings fill the air, and I'm paralyzed. When Luke's distinctive voice sweeps over the room, the universe stops again.

It's time to tell you how I feel
I know you've been waiting
I know you've been wondering when

It's time to let go of the past
There's nothing but heartache
Nothing worth keeping now

I want to give you the world
And all that I have
I want to make you my baby
To have and to hold
I want to give you my word
I'll never let go
I'll never let go

I, I won't give you up
Cause I don't want to live without you by my side
Forevermore I want you always
As long as I'm alive
I'll have you 'til the end of time

I won't ever let you go
Cause I want you always
I want you always always

When life gets harder than we planned
I promise I'll listen
I promise I'll do whatever it takes
Cause I, I don't want to waste one single moment
From a silly little mistake

Holland joins him on the second chorus, her perfect harmony turning music into legend. This moment… I can't breathe, can't move, can't do anything but hold Callie and pray nothing ever takes her from me.

I want to give you the world
And all that I have
I want to make you my baby
To have and to hold
I want to give you my word
I'll never let go
I'll never let go

I, I won't give you up
Cause I don't want to live you without you by my side
Forevermore
I want you always
As long as I'm alive
I'll have you 'til the end of time
I won't ever let you go
Cause I want you always

I want you always.

The room is silent when the last notes of the song ring out, except for the sound of sniffs and tears. And not even ours. No, because we're buried in each other, hiding from everyone else to share this incredible moment privately.

"I'm yours. Always," I whisper against her lips.

She kisses me back, locking me in place. Yeah, I get that this part is supposed to come later but there are no rules anymore. We broke them all from the moment we met.

"Casey?"

"Yeah?"

"Nothing matters. Just us."

"Always."

∞∞∞∞

I'm trying to pay attention to the rest of the ceremony. I really am. It's my surprise, impromptu wedding after all, but after Callie's song, the only part that seems to matter is that moment we get the rings and Pastor Jim declares that we're man and wife. Plus, there's Derrick.

"What's he doing?" I whisper to Callie as Pastor Jim continues blabbing on about something related to First Corinthians.

She follows my gaze to Derrick who's going from guest to guest, shoving something in their faces.

"I think he's collecting signatures," she whispers back.

"For a petition to run for office? What?"

She squints toward the latest victim. "Nope. Our guest book. He's taking his job very seriously."

Pastor Jim gives me a hard look when I snicker, and I bite the inside of my cheek. *Sorry,* I mouth.

"May we have the rings, please?"

Luke produces them from his pocket, nailing his role as Best Man. Maid of Honor too the way he winks at Callie as he hands them to the pastor.

"These rings symbolize…" *Blah, blah, blah.* Callie smiles up at me, and I'm pretty sure she's just as distracted as I am. Hopefully, someone's filming this part too.

I've played stages, arenas, stadiums, and here's my hand, shaking like a jackhammer when it's forced to take a tiny platinum band from Pastor Jim's hand. What's with the microscopic design anyway?

Come on, dude. You got this. Pretend it's a drum key.

Callie squeezes my other hand, probably trying to calm me down. Damn, I wish we'd practiced this. Wedding rehearsals aren't the bullshit I'd thought. I'm supposed to say something too. Everyone's staring at me. Pastor Jim keeps nodding toward me like that's going to help me remember what the hell I'm supposed to do now.

"With this ring…" he whispers, urging me on.

"With this ring," I repeat. He stares at me. I stare at him. Callie chuckles.

"I give you…" he says.

"I give you."

No, that doesn't sound right. There has to be more. *C'mon brain. Feel free to join in at any moment.*

"My love, my life, and my heart…"

Right. That. "My love, my life, and my heart."

Good job, Case.

"Callie?" he says, turning toward my bride.

Of course Callie who's never been onstage a day in her life takes the ring like a pro and shoves it on my finger.

"Casey, with this ring I give you my love, my life, and my heart."

Pastor Jim is smiling. Everyone is. Wait, is this the part where I kiss her? No. Maybe?

"Do I—"

Okay, nope. He's still talking. Something about journeys and footsteps and other shit that doesn't let me kiss my girl. Why is she so freaking beautiful? That simple platinum band on her finger is the most gorgeous thing I've ever seen. I run my thumb over it, wondering what it will be like to relive this moment every time I touch it. My wife. My *wife!*

"And now, with the power vested in me by the Holy Christian Church and the state of Texas, I now pronounce you husband and wife. You may demonstrate your union with a kiss."

Score! This part I can do. I barely hear the requisite catcalls and teasing from the crowd as I pull my *wife!* into my arms. Huge hazel eyes stare up at me, bright with anticipation. Her lips part, waiting, and I swear my throat closes up. We've kissed hundreds, thousands of times, but this one… This one.

I stare at her lips, tracing them gently with my finger.

"I will never stop kissing you," I whisper.

"Good," she says through a smile.

I lean in, and the lobby of the Florecita Hotel erupts into cheers and applause. The commotion is nothing compared to the fireworks exploding in my head, sending sparks through every vein in my body. My love. My life. My heart.

Forever, Cal.

"Until zombies do us part," she whispers back.

23: SATURDAY 11:03AM

Wow. So many donuts. Colorful rows form fields of sugar in an auxiliary ballroom the hotel must have freed up for us. Nowhere near enough room for the two hundred souls crammed inside, even with the standing-room-only setup. But for a last-minute donut and coffee reception, it's not half-bad. I still can't believe so many people came out for an impromptu early morning non-wedding wedding. Plus, my wife's face (*my wife!!!*) when she sees the fully-loaded tea bar is enough to make a new husband weep. Then again, so's Derrick's unadulterated bliss. He looks ready to toss himself into the sea of pastries.

"Duuude," he whispers reverently.

"All you, man," I say, waving him toward the bounty.

"Wait, don't the bride and groom go first?"

"I think that's for birthdays. Callie's busy anyway." I nod toward the tea table where she stands frozen with indecision. Damn she's cute, biting her lip with that perplexed awe. "Excuse me," I say to Derrick whose plate is already stacked. Wow, that was fast.

I'm laser-focused as I return several greetings and well-wishes on my way to the Tea Queen. She jumps when I snake my arms around her from behind and pull her to my chest. "So many choices," I murmur against her ear. "What's it gonna be, Mrs. Barrett?"

She twists a grin back at me. "I could be here all day."

"The first thing we're doing when we get our own place is setting up a tea station for you."

"Really?" Those eyes. Damn. I can't.

"Really. Whatever you want, babe. *Everything* you want." I kiss her hair, swaying our bodies to the rhythm of Jesse's guitar over in the corner. That kid's voice elevates even a donut reception to the next level.

"I think I might start with the Paris Blend. Do you think it's actually from Paris?"

No clue, but the way she says it makes me pray that it is.

"I don't know. Bet it's delicious though. You hungry? I'll grab you a donut before Derrick eats them all."

She casts a disgusted look at the table where Eli and Sweeny have joined Derrick in their quest to rid the planet of all pastries.

"Sure. Just a glazed one, please."

"You got it."

It's freaking hard to let her go, but right now I'm less important than whatever "Paris Blend" is anyway. Besides, a storm's brewing. I feel it in the air with my sixth sense for family drama.

"Nestor Barrett, you put that back!" Ms. Hawthorne shouts, right on cue. She launches an indignant point at her beau. "You know what the doctor said about your cholesterol!"

"Donuts don't have cholesterol," Nestor counters.

"Of course they do! Everything has cholesterol," she huffs.

"Celery?"

"Pfft." But her head is doing the math. Nestor crosses his arms with all the smugness of a spoiled royal.

"Carrots?" he continues. "Romaine lettuce? Iceberg lettuce? Batavia lettuce?"

"Fine! None of the lettuces! But there are no Batavian lettuce donuts on that table, are there? Are there!"

Nestor grumbles something about ranch dressing before grabbing a sugar-coated donut and marching off, a furious Ms. Hawthorne chasing after him.

"How you feeling?" Luke asks, pulling up beside me.

"Good, man. Really good." The smile in my chest can't even be quelled by Uncle Nestor today. "What you did for us…" I shake my head, willing the tears to stop before they hit my throat. I'm not going to be that guy. But when Luke's gaze softens with a lifetime of brotherhood, there's no hope for me. I swat at my eyes and pull him into a hug. "I love you, bro. Thank you."

"I love you too, Case. We couldn't be happier for you and Cal."

I nod, pulling back before I totally lose my shit.

"Anyway, it wasn't just me," he continues, slapping my shoulder. "It took all of us to pull this off. Holland, especially."

"She's amazing. You struck gold too, man. Hey…" I squint around the room, scanning the guests. "Where is she anyway? I'm sure Callie wants to thank her."

"Um…" Luke quiets. Wait, is he blushing?

"Okay, dude. What the hell is going on with your girlfriend?"

He bites his lip, gaze darting to the door. "She'd kill me."

"Why? She have some weird foreign stomach flu or something?"

"Well, no. Not exactly."

I shrug. "Okay. Well, I'll just send Callie to go chat with her and find out."

"No! I mean…" He pulls me close and leans toward my ear. "She's pregnant, dude."

Waiiiiiit…..

The shout forms. Rising, there it is, rushing from my lungs, up through my throat and—

"Shh!" Luke says with a laugh. "You can't tell anyone."

"What? Why the hell not? I want to tell everyone!" I whisper-shout, shoving him.

"Because she's not at twelve weeks yet. Plus, she doesn't want to take anything away from you and Callie right now."

"Are you fucking serious? Callie would go nuts if she knew. Wait, does she?"

Luke's eyes widen. "No. And your wedding day will also be your funeral if you tell her. You *have* to let Holland tell her. She's planning to soon."

Maybe I kind of understand Derrick's seal-dance for once. "This rocks, dude. Congrats."

His grin makes me think it's physically painful for him to keep this to himself. "Thanks, man. We're pretty fucking stoked."

I glance back at Callie who still has not chosen a freaking teabag. "Tell Holland she needs to forget this deference bullshit. She has to tell Cal, like, yesterday. That will be the best wedding present you two can possibly give her."

"You think?"

"She's my wife, dude. I *know.*"

∞∞∞∞

Holland's news will have had to wait though, because apparently, our elusive suitor Marty Heilman has one last surprise for us. Jesse's musical artistry fades into silence at the legit trumpet blast announcing the arrival of… something. I can't see over the crowd, but I'm not optimistic. I know it's from Marty because my phone lights up with a text from an unknown number at the same moment.

May the dance of life commence with your new partner.

And commence it does. My groomsmen aggressively clear floor space for the trumpet player to lead—are those people wearing togas?

"What's happening right now?" Callie asks, tucking her arm around mine. I'm sure my face mirrors hers: concern, curiosity, acceptance of the new normal.

"Marty Heilman," I say casually. She nods and sips her tea.

"That the Paris Blend?"

"It's delicious. Want a taste?" She holds the cup up to me.

"No, thanks. Hey look, a cithara."

"A what?"

"Kind of like an ancient guitar."

"Ah. And there's a flute. I know that one."

"Oh yeah. Huh. Ms. Hawthorne must be in heaven," I say with a snicker.

Callie's brow scrunches into adorable creases. "Uncle Nestor's girlfriend? She likes flutes?"

"Long story."

The dancers are set, and damn they take their job seriously. By their grave expressions, they really are about to perform for the emperor of Rome. The rich twang of the cithara fills the room with its eerie cry. When the flute joins in, the handful of dancers begin undulating in all kinds of strange snake-like maneuvers. What's the protocol for watching Roman-style dancing? I'm not the only one confused, it seems, as I look around the room. Some nod sternly, as if this is the tenth such performance they've been forced to endure this week. Others participate with some off-tempo silent clap that reminds me of Grammy Barrett in the front row of my violin recitals. Cal just looks perplexed.

The other problem with surprise Roman-style wedding dance routines is that no one knows when they end. After the third applause that dies from more oblivious undulation, we stop trying to guess. The cithara though? Pretty cool. Kinda want one. Wonder if I can just order that shit online?

I study the musician's fingers as they pluck and glide over the strings. He's doing something with his other hand too. What is that? I take a step closer, but the dancers keep blocking my view. Another step. And another. And then—

I'm dancing. Well, I'm being led in circles by the hand anyway. The formations seem way more intricate when you're being shoved from one toga-body to the next and expected to… I don't know. Probably not scowl like I currently am. I keep trying to escape, only to be pulled back and surrounded by some *freaking scrappy* dancers, it turns out. And then I see it. My groomsmen. Snickering at first, and then full on belly-laughing when they see they've got my attention.

"You did this?" I mouth, pointing at them. The glee escalates to unseemly levels, and I manage to wrestle myself away from my costumed captors.

"You idiots. You're Marty Heilman?" I say, charging toward them. They back up as far as the crowd will allow. The Limelight guys are laughing so hard I worry for their health. My own band is doubled over, even Luke who I thought was my kin. "Et tu, Brute?" I bark out, shoving him. His smirk only grows. "You losers are taking every one of those damn flower arrangements back to your rooms!"

Apparently this amuses them even more, and by now, we've totally interrupted the weird Roman thing. I can't believe this. Except, I totally believe this. Idiots. A smile plays on my lips as I shake my head. Fucking brilliant idiots who even helped me get arrested with that birds' nest fiasco. Ever want to hug a person and deck them at the same time?

"You should see your face, dude," Derrick cries, seal-clap-jumping.

"Yeah? Does it look like I'm gonna beat the shit out of you while you sleep?"

"You don't even have a key to my room!" he calls back, totally missing the point as usual.

"Just sayin' you all better watch your backs on tour," I bark, adding emphatic points at each of them to offset the smile on my face. When Callie winds her arm around my side, chuckling sweetly, I know it's over. The dudes won Wedding Gifting.

"I can't believe that was them this whole time. And Luke." She lets go of me to shove her BFF. Luke reels back in dramatic acceptance. Callie goes in for the kill and screams when he grabs her. Lifting her off the ground, his smile is downright devilish as she smacks his back. "Luke!" she cries, legs kicking and arms flailing.

"Casey!" she shouts over to me, pleading. I wave back, enjoying her glare. "You're going to let him do this to your wife?"

"Do what?"

"This!"

Luke laughs and sets her down. "Anyway, you can't prove a thing," he teases.

"No? There's no way those idiots came up with all that poetic crap," she says. I flinch along with him at the finger jutting into his ribs. Been there. The girl can jab like nobody's business. Pretty sure even the Roman dance troupe winces at her follow-up attack when he shows zero remorse for his role.

Luke throws his arms over his head, laughing while my wife demonstrates her contempt for Marty Heilman. In a week of insanity, this might be the funniest part.

"You're just going to stand there?" Callie pauses long enough to scold me.

"You seem to have everything under control, babe."

The break must have been enough to calm the adrenaline, because soon she's all smiles and blushes tucked under Luke's arm. I'm about to demand my wife back when she freezes, all humor draining from her face.

I turn and follow her gaze through what suddenly becomes a portal to hell. Well, a demon lair anyway, because there they are, sneering at us with the smugness of groupies who snuck past security.

"What the fuck are you doing here?" I snap. Officer Andy be damned; I have no problem going back to prison for this asshole. Two steps forward, and I find myself rooted for a fight.

"Hey. Not worth it, man," Luke soothes, his arm locked across my chest. Sweeny has my other side, and even Eli grips my shoulder from behind when I struggle to get free.

"Casey, don't." This plea I can't ignore. Not with those hazel eyes filled with fear for me. "Please. I don't want to lose you right now." I pull in a deep breath, limbs shaking, blood pounding. Would I kill Roger Roland? No. Would I get a real hit in? Hell yeah. My vacation to a jail cell at least earned me that.

But Callie.

My wife.

Where's security, anyway?

"What are you doing here, Dad?" Callie asks, stepping between us. I've never seen those perfect brows knitted with so much contempt before.

Slender fingers that playfully attacked Luke a second ago are now balled into small fists at her sides as she leans toward her father, venom in her gaze.

"Of course I'd want to see my only child's wedding."

Roger releases his trashy date to better engage in the battle, and I stiffen. The band's grip on me tightens.

"She's got this," Luke whispers. Does zilch to soothe my rage, but the appearance of security helps.

Callie holds up her hand. "Just a sec, Lee and Tom."

Lee and Tom? Of course she knows the names of tonight's security guys. Her eyes narrow back on her father.

"You are not welcome here. Nor are you welcome in our present or our future. Next time you show up in our lives uninvited, you will have a hell of a lot more than some angry words to deal with. Do you understand?"

Something flickers over his gnarled face. Hesitation? Uncertainty? I get the feeling he's surprised by this side of Callie as well.

"I asked you a question!" she roars, stepping forward.

He flinches and clears his throat. "I was just—"

"No," she hisses, pointing again. "No words other than 'yes, I understand.'"

His gaze darts to me, to my friends, to security, to the crowd of witness, and back to Callie.

"I understand."

"Good."

He starts to back away.

"Oh, and while you're at it. I'd suggest dropping those bullshit charges against Casey or I'll tell the world about Pittsburgh."

"You wouldn't."

"I damn well would."

I've never seen a grown man pale like that. Dude looks ready to hurl as he grabs Whats-Her-Name's arm and drags her after him to the exit.

"Yeah, that's right!" Derrick shouts after him, air-punching a vicious strike.

Stunned silence follows. Callie seething, me in shock, and Eli… snickering?

I glance over at my bandmate who has a grin on his face.

"What is it?" I ask.

He bites his lip. "Callie just said 'bullshit.'"

24: SATURDAY 1:17PM

Callie's asleep when my phone buzzes with a call. As much as I would've loved to celebrate our marriage with all-the-consummation the second we got back to our room, it didn't take a genius to see that she was exhausted. Me? I was still too fired up to rest and decided to guard my wife while she slept. I'll be damned if anyone is going to disturb her.

But here we are, my eternal soul in peril as I stare at Derrick's name on my phone. Now what?

As carefully as possible, I inch off the bed and tiptoe toward the exit. I hate how loud hotel doors are. You'd think a place designed for sleeping would invest in doors that don't sound like a 19th century bank vault.

By the time I get out to the hall, Derrick's call is on its third round of rings.

"What?" I snap.

"Casey?"

"Yeah. What is it?"

"Um..."

Now he's silent?

"Derrick, I swear, if you interrupted me for no reason—"

"No, I have a reason. A good one."

"Which is?"

"Well… You see…"

"Derrick!"

"I might've lost Uncle Nestor."

…

…

"What?"

"Yeah. I mean, I was escorting him and Mrs. H back to their room after our couple's massage and—"

"Hang on. Couple's massage?"

"Yeah, it was Mrs. H's idea. She had a coupon, so we thought—"

"You know what? No. I don't want to know. Just, back to Nestor, please."

"Okay, so I was escorting them home, and Uncle Nestor said he wanted a beer."

"He's not supposed to drink."

"That's what I said!"

Silence.

More silence.

"And?"

Derrick clears his throat. "Oh. Right. So he insisted, and what was I supposed to do? He's my uncle, right?"

"No. He's really not."

"Well, you know what I mean. My surrogate uncle."

"Not a thing."

"And I couldn't say no. The way he gives you those grandpa puppy eyes?"

"Also not a thing."

"Well, he does. And so I said fine. I'd just leave him at the bar, take Mrs. H back to her room, and then go back for Uncle Nestor."

Well, shit. I see where this is going.

"So of course when we got to the room, Mrs. H insisted I watch *Gardens of Love* with her—" (okay, maybe not there)— "and oh my god it was so good, Case. I couldn't leave until I knew if Esmerelda and Hector would be able to convince her father to give up the cattle ranch. It belonged to Ezzy's mother's family so it should have been hers anyway, not—"

"Dude. Nestor!"

"Oh, right. So when I got back to the bar, he was gone."

Air filters through my nostrils in a heavy inhale. "Okay, well, did you ask the bartender?"

"Of course."

…

…

"And?"

"He said he didn't remember him."

"He didn't remember a cantankerous old guy in his bar at one o'clock in the afternoon?"

"Cantankerous, heh."

"Derrick!"

"Right, he didn't. Well, probably because the bar wasn't open when I dropped him off which means the bartender wasn't on duty. Geez, it wasn't even noon. Place was all dark and shit."

My forehead finds the wall. Once. Twice. Three times in a silent bang that would be way more aggressive if Callie wasn't sleeping on the other side. "D, can I ask you something?"

"Sure, man."

"Why would you leave my uncle sitting at a bar that wasn't open?"

…

…

"Right. Huh. That doesn't make sense, does it."

"No."

"Shit. I'm sorry, man."

Clenching my eyes shut, I draw in another deep breath. "Okay. Where are you now?"

"Looking for Nestor."

"Okay, but where?"

"In the bar. I just told you."

Patience, Casey. "Okay. Don't move. I'm on my way."

"Cool, thanks. Want me to order something for you?"

"What? No! We're not hanging out, man. We're going to find my uncle."

"Oh sure, I know. Just thought maybe we could do some Search Party Pre-gaming."

"Um, yeah. D?"

"What?"

"That's definitely, definitely not a thing."

∞∞∞

Derrick paces the hotel bar entrance like he lost my newborn baby, not my seventy-year-old uncle. Fingers tearing at his hair, he looks downright broken shuffling around in assertive arcs.

"Case, man, he was right there. *Right* there," he says, pointing to the last stool at the bar.

"Okay, calm down. Walk me through this."

"Right, so we came here." He stops by the large, open entrance to the bar area and spreads his arms. His face scrunches into thought before he slides about three inches to the right. "Maybe it was here. Wait… no."

"So not that much detail. What happened after you got to bar?"

He seems uncertain about leaving the exact starting location unresolved when he swings toward the bar. "Well, it was roped off, right? Wasn't open. We ducked under the rope—" he demonstrates ducking—"then I helped him onto this stool. Dude had to sit on a stool too. Insisted. Something about Korea."

"Korea?"

"Maybe it was Cambodia. Or Croatia."

"None of those makes sense."

"Okay, well I don't know. There was a reason. Had to be this stool too." He kicks the base, which earns him an annoyed look from the patron currently inhabiting said stool.

"Sorry," I mutter to the guy who turns back to his drink. "Then what?" I say to Derrick, pulling him away before he assaults any other innocent bystanders.

"That's the last I saw him. When I came back, the stool was empty. Well, empty of Uncle N. That guy was there." He casts a cold glare at the stranger as if it's his fault my uncle ran off. I see Derrick's brain working and it scares me.

"Well, I think we can be pretty confident that 'that dude' has nothing to do with Nestor's disappearance."

"But how do you *know*?" Derrick whisper-hisses, all conspiratorial. His eyes, usually curious and round, now look almost beady as they dart to the guy in Nestor's stool.

"Call it Nephew Intuition."

He nods gravely like I didn't just make that up.

"Look, you've spent the most time with him over the last couple of days. What seemed to interest him about the hotel? Did he mention anything he wanted to do? He doesn't have a car or trust public transportation so he's probably still on the premises."

Derrick rubs his chin and resumes pacing. For the briefest of seconds, he almost looks scholarly. Then he says, "how do you feel about lobsters?"

∞∞∞∞

Apparently Derrick has a debilitating fear of lobsters, which is why he refused to take the older couple to view the tanks at the hotel steakhouse yesterday. His current theory is that the bar story was an elaborate ploy by Nestor to sneak away and check out those suckers on his own. Sadly, it's as likely a possibility as any, so here I am, trying to convince the host I don't want a table, just a quick peek at the crustacean tank.

"Sir?"

"I know. Just, I'm looking for my uncle and think he might be here."

"At the lobster tank?"

I strain for a look behind him, hoping I can see the tank from this vantage point. No luck.

"Maybe?"

I feel the man's skepticism, even share it, but after this past week, I'm in no mood to be thwarted no matter how stupid my mission.

We stare each other down until finally he steps back and waves me in with clear disapproval. I'm not sure what kind of mischief he fears at two in the afternoon, but alas, I swallow my pride and scan the restaurant for any sign of a cranky old man and/or lobsters.

After a brief search, I find the lobsters but no old man. "Is that the only lobster tank?" I ask a passing server.

"Yup."

"Thanks," I say, defeated. The server eyes me and my disappointment with suspicion. "My uncle loves lobsters," I explain to make it worse.

She nods, kind of polite. "We have the best in town."

"Oh no, not to eat them. Just to look."

She nods again, not as polite. "I see."

"Right. Um, thanks." I beeline for the exit and Derrick's waiting distress.

"Did you find the lobsters?" he asks the second I come into view.

"Yeah, but no Nestor."

"Damn," he mutters, genuinely surprised. "Thought for sure it'd be the lobsters. Do they have other shellfish tanks?"

I shake my head and start walking. "Let's go. Where else? Think."

Okay, now it's starting to look painful for him.

"I'm such an idiot! What if we never find him?"

I can't believe I'm comforting someone over the loss of my uncle. With a pat on the arm, I reassure him that there's no chance that a lucid adult could be lost in a hotel for all of eternity. I pull away and start moving again before he can hug me.

"Wait!"

I freeze at Derrick's cry and watch his face light up with all-the-thoughts.

"You've got something?" I encourage when he hesitates.

He seems to reconsider under the pressure. "Yeah but he's allergic to pine nuts so never mind."

I don't ask.

My phone buzzes, and I glance down. Molly.

Crap.

"'Sup, sis?"

"Casey, um. I'm sorry to bother you but Nate's not picking up."

"What is it?"

"Well…" She pauses, and I hear the echoes of shouts in the background.

"You okay?" I press.

"Me? Yeah, I'm fine. It's just… can you come down to the indoor pool area?"

Fuck. "Right now? I'm kind of in the middle of something."

"I know, but it's an emergency. I wouldn't ask if it weren't important. It's about Uncle Nestor."

"On my way."

I grab Derrick's arm and drag him toward the elevators.

∞∞∞∞

For the love of all things holy.

Families rush from the pool room, parents still shielding their children's eyes and muttering horrified protests. I feel the need to do the same when I see why.

"Fuck, Uncle Nestor. What are you doing?"

I grab a stack of towels and rush toward the hot tub at the far left wall. Derrick's right behind me, gasping and huffing.

"Dude, he's bare-ass naked!"

"I'm aware of that, Derrick," I growl. "Here, hold these up." I toss him a few of the towels and together we form a protective barrier for the rest of humanity. You're welcome, human race.

"What are you all huffy-puff about?" the old man snaps.

"Gee, I don't know. How could you think any of this would be okay?"

"Well, I fancied a soak. You didn't say to pack swim trunks on the invitation." His gaze narrows sharply to hammer home the fact that this is my fault.

"I really didn't think I needed to. Will you get out of the tub before I get arrested for a second time this weekend?"

Molly stands guard at the entrance, nibbling her fingernails and looking less amused than she was by the fruit-fight the other day. "Will you hurry up? Get him out before we get caught," she fires over at me. Again, because this is my fault?

"Now, Uncle Nestor," I say, ready to wade into the water and drag him out.

"Please, Uncle N?" Derrick is more conciliatory, even crouching down by the ledge to plead with him at eye level. Something changes in the hard, old man, and he swats the water in defeat.

"Oh, fine," he grumbles, pushing up and sloshing toward the stairs. I avert my gaze to the ceiling, hoping I never have to see my uncle naked again.

"Where are your clothes?" I ask, glancing around the room.

He's quiet as Derrick wraps several towels around him, turning him into a bitter, hairy mummy.

"You," I say to Derrick when I get no response from Nestor. "Can I trust you to get him back to his room?"

"What about his clothes?"

"We'll figure that out later. Or better yet, have Reece and Jay help you look. But Derrick."

"Yeah?"

"If you call me again with an Uncle Nestor emergency, I'll be kicking you off the tour, got it?"

His eyes go round, big and alarmed as he nods slowly.

I'm not even joking. I know for a fact that Jay is also an excellent drummer.

Molly has her fingers laced over her head when I turn back. She watches the strange parade with the same skepticism I feel.

"How are we related to him?" she mutters.

I almost laugh. "You kidding? That'll be us in fifty years."

She groans and covers her face. "Don't tell me that."

I'm not ready to let her off the hook. "So where's Eli? Trouble in paradise?"

She doesn't appreciate my humor. "I don't think it's going to work out."

"No? Why's that?" Partly I'm curious. Mostly I like hearing how right I am about shit.

With a huff, she crosses her arms, though I can tell there's some pent-up steam just waiting to blow. She's not so mad that I asked. "Because…" She shakes her head. Ready. Aim. Fire!

"Oh my gosh! We went for Italian and, Casey, he asked for two extra knives. Know why?"

"I'm going to guess not to butter lots of bread?"

"No. He wanted to use them like chopsticks to eat his spaghetti. He said that's how they do it in Italy."

"Huh." A smile tugs at my lips the longer I let my brain work on that image.

"Yeah, and then he said he was pretty sure Lithuania and Lichtenstein were the same country. He didn't even know Andorra existed. Haven't you guys toured Europe, like, a million times?"

"Not quite a million."

"Oh! And he asked for half a glass of water, no ice, then used it to rinse his fork before eating something else. Who does that?"

"Eli."

"And who asks the server if she's single *while* on a date with another woman?"

"Eli."

"And then orders a pizza to go *for later with the guys*?"

"Eli."

"And doesn't even say anything when we get back to the hotel? Just gives the peace sign and walks off with his stupid pizza?"

"Eli."

This huff is more aggressive, and I work to suppress my amusement.

"So not marriage material?" I ask, somehow managing to keep a straight face.

Molly responds with a mic-drop glare she must have learned from Callie.

25: SATURDAY 3:59PM

Turns out finding Uncle Nestor skinny-dipping in a public pool was just the beginning of my nightmare afternoon. I'd no sooner gotten Derrick refocused on Nestor duty when more rumors from Aunt Norma started a queue of panic on my phone.

No, I haven't run off to South America.

Yes, Callie and I are married for real; this isn't a hoax.

No, she's not pregnant with someone else's baby; not mine either; damn it, she's not pregnant! Yes I'm sure!

My mom wanted—needed—family pictures right now, no buts, she gave birth to me after all and doesn't that earn her a silly picture? Nothing could dissuade her. Not even the fact that the rest of the family were missing, and after spending forty-five minutes trying to round them up from around the resort, she finally settled for a selfie with me. Tomorrow's a better day for pictures anyway, according to her.

Uncle Alan decided to check out early. Why's that my problem? Why wouldn't it be? Everything's my fucking problem, apparently, including the issue he had with his bill. Required my direct attention, and after much debate, came down to a misunderstanding about how room service works. Also *Blanche* dumped him, which explains why he's extra ornery.

As if all of that wasn't enough, at some point that afternoon Uncle N and Ms. Hawthorne also broke up. Then they reconciled, broke up, and reconciled again. This required my attention as well—mostly for Derrick who needed crisis counseling at the prospect of his favorite non-relatives' near split.

By the time I trudge back to my room, my heart is as sluggish as my body. We're a minute away from our original ceremony time and I'd wanted to do something special with Callie to acknowledge it. Instead, I'll be lucky if she doesn't slug me for abandoning her moments after getting married.

Slipping my key in the door, I move inside, wondering if she's still asleep. The lights are dimmed but not off like they were when I left. Something else is different as well. The smell maybe? Not quite as sickeningly floral. A quick scan of the foyer and I realize it's been cleared of all flower vomit. Guess Callie got as fed up with the forest as I was.

"Sorry, babe. It's been a nightmare of an afternoon. I didn't mean to be gone—"

I freeze.

Stretched out on the bed in some silky black contraption is an angel. Scratch that—a goddess. She's magnificent lying there, watching me with a mischievous look I want to lick off her face. Is she trying to kill me?

"Don't think I forgot it's our wedding night," Callie says with all the sass that barely there lace requires.

I swallow, still trying to catch my breath. She looks serious, determined even, but after this week, I trust nothing. Her finger moves in enticing arcs, encouraging me forward. I only make it a few steps before she's slinking off the bed, prowling toward me.

"Don't," she says, when I reach for the hem of my shirt.

My hand stalls and lowers at her warning look.

"You've spent the last week taking care of everyone else, Casey Barrett." Her tone is stern; her gaze, fixed. "It's time for someone to take care of you."

Damn.

My blood thumps loudly in my veins, my body already hard and tense. Her fingers lift the edge of my t-shirt above the waist of my jeans, just enough to make my breath hitch. Maybe there's a small groan when she traces the exposed skin over my abs. She's killing me. Damn near destroying me right now.

Her hands match the aggression in her eyes as she pushes her palms up my chest, dragging my shirt with them. Yanking it over my head, she uses it to lock my arms behind me. Hell yeah, I let her shove me to the bed. My body has been splashed on covers and websites around the world but only one woman gets access. And my girl? Full VIP privileges.

I wait, propped up on my elbows, not daring to move. I've never seen her look so hungry, so intent. The dim lighting is enough to highlight every perfect curve of her body as she moves toward me. Slowly. Watching. Tracing every line of my chest with lust.

"You are so hot," she whispers, and yeah, that makes me grin. "And your smile…" She shakes her head as she climbs onto the bed. Straddling my hips, she sinks hard, forcing a hiss from me. "And you're so talented. So good and sweet and…"

I close my eyes, trying to stay balanced with her fingers sinking into my skin, massaging, tempting, taking what they want. Her left hand snakes around my neck and twists into my hair.

She pulls my head back. "Look at me."

I do, my gaze locked on hers.

"I'm so lucky," she says quietly, tracing my lips with her other hand. Yeah, I officially became a mess four seductions ago. Now? I'm her captive. A toy in her hands. Hers to have, hold, and enjoy because heaven knows it doesn't get any better than this.

Her hips circle hard and slow on my dick, and I gasp in a breath. And I'm sorry. I can't hold back anymore.

I slide out of the shirt and grip her face in my hands, forcing her kisses to collide with mine. Have you ever wanted to consume someone? Pull them into your soul and hold them there until their beauty shines out of you too? That's Callie for me. Has been since the day we met. Will be until the day I die because this, right here, isn't sex. This is love, trust, loyalty, friendship, selflessness, compassion, and every good thing about being human. This is happiness.

And this is what happens when you find your dream and marry the shit out of her.

26: SUNDAY 7:35AM

I wake to the sweetest smile inches from mine. It's almost painful how it burrows into my heart.

"Morning, Mrs. Barrett," I mumble, my own lips twisting into a smile.

"Morning, Mr. Barrett."

She turns so I can tuck her against me. Autopilot, this maneuver. I close my eyes again, so content I could probably sleep for another five hours like this. And yeah, maybe I'm still tired from last night because damn that was epic. Making love was just the beginning of Callie's plans for me. A sensual massage and another heated round of couples-play later, we were finally sated enough for the real party: battling it out with killer insects in the new Atomic Titans game. Yes, my goddess had arranged to have my gaming system set up and spent the rest of the night allowing me to teach her how to play the newest release of my favorite series. Not that I ever doubted our love for a second, but after hours of watching her adorable pout while attempting to blow up alien insects, it's pretty much cemented for all of eternity. Callie Roland

Barrett is the queen of my heart—even if she's not the greatest Arachnid Slayer of all time.

"I still can't believe Holland and Luke are pregnant," she says now, just as awed as the eighteen times she said it last night. Once our own baby-making had died down, it was all about Holland and Luke. Apparently, Holland had stopped by during my Nestor hunt the previous afternoon to share the news. Yep, there's nothing like talking baby showers and registries when you're elbow deep in insect guts. "Did you know that's why she hasn't been able to eat broccoli lately?" By her tone, this information solves at least half the world's mysteries.

"I didn't know she hasn't been eating broccoli lately."

"Well, she hasn't. And also, she said she can't be in the same room as cottage cheese."

"Hmm… neither can I. Maybe I'm pregnant too?"

Callie shoves me, and I wrestle her against me to prevent a second attack. Okay, so that's not the only reason. She settles into my embrace, and maybe a small, tiny part of my brain starts to imagine her pregnant with my baby one day.

"What time's brunch again?" I ask, hoping the answer is never. I'd also take: *let's have sex ten more times.*

She shakes her head. "We talked about this. We're calling it Breakfast Club."

"Call it what you want, it's still a glorified welcoming brunch."

"Um, the wedding's over, genius. If anything, it would be a goodbye brunch."

"Fine. What time's the goodbye brunch?"

"You mean Breakfast Club?"

She shrieks when my fingers find the ticklish spot just blow her ribs.

∞∞∞

My wife was right.

I suppose I'll have to get used to saying that frequently in the future. I can't say the small banquet room looks exactly like Jemma's, the café where we met, but the smell of French toast (with just the right amount of powdered sugar) definitely takes us back to the moment it all began. We're a little late, so the room is already full of our nearest and dearest. Luke, Holland, Jesse, Sweeny, Eli, Nate, Molly, god I can't even take it all in. So many people who love us enough to share this moment. To create the magic that was yesterday and make my life the rich blessing it's become. It's still surreal as they applaud, their faces bright and beaming, reflecting our love for them. Gotta say, it's not easy to keep that lump of emotion in my chest, and when I glance over at Cal, her eyes are glistening.

"You okay, babe?" I whisper, pulling her against my side.

Her teeth sink into her lip as she nods, but I'm pretty sure this is about the smile peeking through. "Can you believe it?"

"What?"

"Everything." She wipes at her eyes, and I press a kiss to her hair. "One moment, one conversation in a little café brought us here. Fate is a funny thing, huh?"

"Fate? No, babe. This"—I motion around the room—"is all you."

She looks up, face shining. "Well, shortly before I met Luke someone told me: never curb your compassion. I've tried to live by that ever since."

"Really, wow." Studying my wife's warm expression, I can't think of a better description for Callie Roland Barrett. She brought us here. Saved more than one life the day she chose compassion in a shitty downtown diner. She made an impact that will live on for decades to come, and I'm freaking honored she chose me. And man, I can't wait to watch her change the world. I'm in awe of this woman, the love of my life, my everything. I don't even have the words to express how much I love her, but I plan to spend the rest of my days showing it.

However, all of that will have to wait because, "Shit. Please tell me Derrick isn't naked under that rock shawl…"

THE END

POSTLUDE

Several weeks later…

So many kitchen gadgets. Callie scans the floor of gifts beside me, probably thinking the same thing. "Wow, we really need to get a kitchen. What do you think this one does?" She holds up a machine that looks like a cross between a medieval torture device and a vibrator.

"No clue. What does the box say?"

She scans the text and pictures. "Well it looks like it does something with avocado. I love avocado."

"Then avocados you shall have."

She grins and adds it to the pile. I glance over at her notepad as she writes: *Grace and Pat, the avocado crusher thing.*

Heh.

I pull another package from the stack of unopened gifts and peel off the envelope. Inside is the most flowery message and font I've ever seen. It's so bad I start to break a sweat amidst graphic Marty Heilman flashbacks. The card is signed

Uncle Nestor and Ms. Hawthorne, though. I'm going to lean heavily on Ms. Hawthorne's role in this.

"Uncle Nestor and Ms. Hawthorne," I say to Callie who jots it down. By her look, she's not entirely confident about this gift either. I rip off the paper that looks like it was manufactured four decades ago and has been used several times before. The worn garment box beneath it looks the same.

I suck in a breath as I remove the lid. Should have let Callie take this one.

Funny how you can be shocked and totally not at the same time. The wrapping and box didn't remotely do justice to the treasures inside. I lift them out with reverence and stretch one in front of us for Callie to appreciate.

"What the heck is that?" she asks. "Did she knit us something? Looks like a matching pair." She bends closer to inspect. "Oh, wow. Our names and the wedding date. Are they small blankets?"

"No." I snort a laugh and sling it around her shoulders. Pretty cute on her, actually. "Duh. It's a rock shawl."

EPILOGUE: EIGHTEEN MONTHS LATER

Epilogue One: Wes

We've played this song hundreds of times. Thousands? Fine, dozens, who the hell knows. The point is you'd think I'd be used to watching Hannah Drake seduce the audience with nothing but her voice and a mic stand. *Make love to the mic*, such a stupid cliché, but yeah, my girl makes the lamest-ass stuff relevant, cool, and fucking sexy.

She was a natural on stage, which surprised no one but her. Certainly not me, although I'll admit I never expected Viper Rising to hit charts so soon. After our debut album went gold two weeks after release, and platinum a month in, the label was talking headlining tours even before we wrapped the first one opening for Tracing Holland. But no matter how many stages we play, how many cities, countries, and venues, it never gets old watching Hannah do what she was born to do. I kind of feel like a dirty bastard ogling my girlfriend from stage left, counting the seconds until we can be alone and I can show her what she does to me. When she shoots me those sexy winks… yeah, I'm done. For two years, we've played that game. Two years of sharing our music and our souls. Which is why after two years, tonight is going to be different.

It's the last show of our Venom tour, so the energy is already high. Sweat soaks my temples, my shirt, pretty much every inch of me after rocking the stage for two hours. Hannah's drenched as well, though you'd never know it. She wears perspiration like a mermaid. Makes her glisten and sparkle and shit. So sue me if my thoughts keep skipping to hot showers and slick skin.

Mermaid, heh. She'd punch me for suggesting it.

"Fangs bared, spring out, out
Of hell, don't tell
Me what I am
I'm not, not your pet
I'm your hidden regret
So hear me, you should fucking fear me
As I rise."

Hell yeah, I hear her. New and different than every other night, too, as my heart pounds and my blood sears through me. She glances over to connect for the final tag, and I feel her in every cell of my body. Those bedroom eyes are just for me; the electric smile is for everyone else. I smile back and belt out the final harmony to bring the tour to its official close.

Even the crowd seems to sense that tonight is special. Their final eruption when the lights flash and the guitars ring out is something for the memory bank. Hannah's expression though? That's fucking otherworldly.

Get it together, Wes. It's supposed to be a surprise.

We duck off the stage when the lights go out and wind toward the exit. Hannah practically squeals once we're clear.

"That was incredible! I can't wait to call Holland."

"Yeah?" I say, handing off my guitar to the tech.

"I told her I'd let her know how it went."

"Your final show on your first headline tour. It's a big moment, babe."

She grins and loops her arms around my chest as we move toward the green room.

"I'm going to remember this forever. I swear, the high right now?"

I smile to myself. *Breathe, dude. Breathe.*

"Right. Pretty sweet, eh?"

"It's amazing! I mean every night is fun, but this…" She shakes her head, and I'd do anything to capture that look for my own mental vault. People write chart-topping songs about that shit.

The door to the green room looms up ahead, slightly ajar as I planned. Hopefully the guys and the crew remembered to steer clear. She's still chatting about the show, but honestly, my brain is already in the dimly lit room ahead. Oh, and I'm fucking terrified.

"You okay?" she asks, drawing me back.

"What? Yeah, of course. Why?"

Her eyes squint with doubt. "You're being quiet."

I shrug. "Tired, I guess. It's been a long month."

"Yeah, I suppose. Oh! Did you get a card for the party tomorrow?"

"Holland's thing? Yeah."

"Great, thanks. I meant to do it when we had that break in Nashville."

"It's fine. Picked up a gift card, too."

"Oh, good. That's perfect. I can't wait to go home. It's been so long."

I squeeze her shoulder. "Yeah, the road is tough. It'll be nice to be home for a little bit."

"Exactly. I'm gonna grab a glass of wine and go straight to the hotel. Early flight!"

"Right," I say. It comes out as more of a gasp which gets her attention.

"You sure you're okay?" she asks.

I manage a nod and pull open the door.

∞∞∞∞

Hannah gasps at the transformation of the green room into an elegant oasis. Not too flowery, mind you. The really romantic shit makes her vomit. Just enough to know something's up and she should be prepared.

"Did you do this?" she asks, fingers brushing her lips as she takes in the details. Her favorite champagne, favorite flowers (tiger lilies), and a large vase filled with her absolute favorite food: sour gummy worms.

"Congratulations, babe. You're incredible." I pull her in for a kiss which turns out to be a mistake. I have a plan, but once her lips respond with all the heat and energy of the last few hours, I'm done. I snake my hands into her hair, deepening our connection until my body is primed and ready for more than what's appropriate in a green room.

"Hold on," I breathe, forcing myself back. Impossible with the way her eyes reflect the candle flames behind me.

Her gaze is all longing and passion and curiosity and all the things that drive me crazy about her.

Still, there's a plan.

I pull in a deep breath and struggle to let her go. Finally, I manage to step away and move to the small safe under the vanity. My hands tremble as I attempt to enter the combination. I feel her suspicious gaze behind me, sense her anticipation. That only ejects me further off my game. Fuck this safe. Should have just kept the ring in my pocket.

Finally, it clicks open, and I pull out the box. After a quick peek to make sure everything's intact, I force myself back around. Hannah already has tears in her eyes, her hands covering her mouth. Damn, she's beautiful. I swallow and open the box.

"Hannah Drake, we've known each other most of our lives. I have no regrets about the paths we've taken because they brought us here to this moment. But what I'm certain of now is that I don't want to continue one more day without you on my journey. If you feel the same, please consider marrying me so we can navigate life together?"

There's no air, no words, as I wait in agony. Her teary gaze travels over my face, to the ring, back to my eyes that have to be pleading at this point. If she says no I think my heart will shatter into a pile of ash right here on the wood floor. If she says yes…? My pulse pounds violently.

She lifts the box from my hand, delicately tracing the treasure inside. Tears slide down her cheeks as she studies the ring. "It's so beautiful," she whispers. "Where did you find it?"

"I had it made for you. Only you."

I force more air into my lungs, praying I know her as well as I thought I did. A black gold snake forms a circle from tale to fangs that almost touch at the top of the ring. I tried to model the snake design as closely to her viper tattoo as possible. The snake's eyes glisten with a unique shine from two small, black diamonds. The ring is understated, astonishing, gorgeous, and intricate, just like it's hopeful wearer.

Please, Hannah, please.

I bite my lip to keep from begging out loud as I wait.

She pulls the ring from the box and slips it on her finger. It's a perfect fit and looks even more beautiful on her hand.

Finally—*finally*—she meets my gaze with a giant grin. Before I can react, she launches herself into my arms, and I jump back to receive her. Relief bubbles out as laughter when I squeeze her against me.

"Of course, Wesley Alton. Let's do this."

EPILOGUE TWO: JESSE

I shake some water from my hair and step out of the shower. Wrapping a towel around my waist, I saunter toward the bedroom where Mila sits at her desk, working as always. Those sexy glasses kill me, though. Wish she'd wear them all the time.

"Oh good, you're done," she says without looking up. "What do you think of this for the press release? 'Jesse Everett and the members of international alternative rock sensation, Limelight, are thrilled to announce the grand opening of Parker's Play Yard—a non-profit campus of entertainment, education, and services benefiting foster children and their families."

A smile spreads over my lips. Huh. There's so much I love about that sentence... and so much I don't. "International alternative rock sensation? Can't we just say 'the guys from Limelight?'"

Apparently not the way her glare shoots back at me. Her expression changes when she notices I'm bare-ass naked. My smile shifts to a grin. "What is it, babe? Aren't you supposed to be working?"

Guess that's a no because now she's moving toward me. She reaches up to remove her glasses, but I stop her.

"Leave them on," I say, capturing her wrists in my grip.

"Why are you so damn sexy? All the freaking time. Ugh." She threads her hands in my wet hair, pressing her hips into mine. Yeah, that's going to be a problem.

"You're killing me, babe," I groan out as she moves in slow aggression.

"Good. Do something about it."

Challenge accepted.

We fall to the bed, where I lean over her on my elbows. She gasps at the pressure of my erection, but it's her own fault. She certainly doesn't help by relocating her attention from my hair to my ass. She claws me in perfect rhythm until I'm hopelessly at her mercy.

"You're still overly dressed," I murmur against her neck. A mischievous spark flashes in her glacial blue gaze. God, her eyes just wreck me. Combine it with that distinctive Mila Taylor snark, and I'm a goner.

"I reckon we should change it up this time," she says, shoving her hands up my back and around my shoulders.

"Yeah?"

Before I know it, I'm on my back, staring up at an insistent vixen. She straddles my hips, forcing my shoulders against the mattress with her palms. I shudder under the intensity of her gaze. The anticipation. She straightens slightly, her fingers scaling the large tattoo covering the left side of my chest, honoring Parker's memory.

"It scares me sometimes how much I feel for you," she says quietly. Her touch moves to my lips where her confession has rendered me mute. "Do you love me?"

I pull in a deep breath. "Ridiculously."

Her grin suddenly infuses with the sensual aggression that drives me crazy.

Send me, wreck me, I won't object to how you affect me. Trigger the pain and let's remain phantoms of tragic desire.

"Tell me," she whispers, leaning close to my ear.

"Tell you what?"

"The poetry in your head. I just saw the cogs turning. I can see it in your eyes."

My breaths are getting more erratic as she works my body. I gasp when she grabs me, massaging in deliberate torture.

"It's nothing," I manage.

She shakes her head, nearly crushing me into the sheets. "Your words are never nothing, love. Your words are my air."

"You just love me for my art."

"No, I love that you *are* your art."

My mouth spreads into a smile as well. "Yeah? Show me how much you love my *art*."

∞∞∞

This is it.

I've played stages around the world, but standing on a tiny platform in front of two hundred people is scaring the hell out of me. I gaze out over the crowd of smiling faces, some familiar, most looking formal and official with fancy press badges. I didn't want any of this, but Mila insisted. "It's necessary for a successful launch," she'd said. I know she's right, but still. Parker would hate the pomp and circumstance as much as I do.

"Thank you, everyone, for coming out to support the Parker Everett Foundation with the opening of Parker's Play Yard," Mila directs into the mic in her crisp, authoritative voice. I swear I could come just listening to her talk sometimes. "On behalf of Jesse Everett and Limelight, we welcome you and officially declare Parker's Play Yard open for operation!"

The crowd applauds, mostly with polite claps, except for the random whoops coming from my right. I shake my head and smile over at Derrick.

There's a ribbon too. Forgot to mention that. Mila hands me giant, stupid-looking scissors, and I wait as Chris takes the other handle so we can photo-op the crap out of this moment. My addiction mentor turned General Manager offers a warm smile, probably sensing my anxiety. So many emotions right now; my heart is racing. My brain is numb.

"He's here with us," she whispers to me.

I swallow the pressure in my throat and force a nod. My pain is my own; I won't cry in front of all these cameras.

My left fist clenches, driving my nails into my palms as we wait for the official all-clear to finish this annoying ceremony. I understand, really, but I'll never get used to this shit. Finally, Mila nods and we squeeze the blades through the ribbon.

Look, Park, we cut a piece of string.

I smirk, imagining my brother rolling his eyes beside me.

More applause at my flawless cutting skills. I guess if the music thing doesn't work out, I could always work a gift-wrapping booth.

"What's so funny?" Mila asks me as the audience starts to disperse and heads into the building.

"Nothing. Just thinking about how much Parker would hate this bullshit."

She gives me a stern look. "Well, it's necessary for the foundation and—"

"—is required for a successful launch. Yeah, yeah, I know."

Her shoulder bumps into mine, but she's smiling again. I tuck my arm around her and turn toward the façade of the building. Located in suburban Philadelphia, the campus is a repurposed office complex that had been abandoned for some time. It wasn't cheap, but with Luke, the other NSB guys, and several high-profile donors, it didn't take long to raise the funds. Parker's Play Yard is a one-stop hub for children and their families, including recreational facilities, counseling services, training programs, and even dormitories for short-term housing.

One day I'd like to fund a full-scale group home for older teens, but Mila says we need to focus on one project at a time. She's the genius behind the business side of PEF. I had zero hesitation to appoint her COO. When she asked who would run Parker's Play Yard, that was a no-brainer as well. I immediately called Chris, my original mentor from EZ Kings who guided me, my father, and countless others on the path to recovery. She accepted and will be the full-time administrator.

"I love you, Jess. You're going to help loads of kids," Mila says, drawing me back to the present. I force a smile, and she kisses me gently. "I better get in there and make sure everything's under control with the launch. Are you gonna be alright?"

"Yeah, I think so," I say, not sure. But she can't help with what's going on inside me. Like usual, I need her to manage our lives while I manage myself. I don't know what I'd do without Mila Taylor. She pretends I'm the prize in our relationship, but the truth is, we're different sides of the same gemstone. And we're rubble without each other. All of that passes between us before she pulls away with another smile.

"Come and find me when you're sorted."

I nod and watch her descend the stairs. The stage is empty now, and only a few spectators linger in conversation among the chairs below.

Just you and me now, Park. What do you think of your legacy?

My gaze passes over the modern yet playful exterior of the building. It looks inviting, the sign over the grand entrance a work of art in itself. Rewind ten years and I would have killed to have access to a place like this. And really, that's what inspired the design. The entire complex is an answer to the question, "What would have saved me from the hell of my childhood?"

"Jesse?"

I flinch and turn at the interruption. Dad approaches, and I lean into his outstretched arms.

"It's amazing, son. Truly remarkable."

"Thanks." I clear my throat. "You should have been onstage with us for the ceremony."

He shakes his head. "Nah, this is your project. Plus, I liked being able to watch from the front row."

I nod, quickly losing the battle I've been fighting since waking up this morning. I promised I wouldn't, but…

"I miss him, Dad. I miss him so much." My voice is little more than a whisper, cracking under the weight of the pain that never goes away. My father's arms tighten around me, and I bury my face in his shoulder like I'm eight years old.

"I know, son. Me too."

"I thought it would stop hurting at some point."

"It will never stop hurting, but because of you and this foundation, the pain can mean something."

I want to believe that. *Philadelphia: the city of brotherly love.* With Parker's memory pushing us on, we've surpassed expectations. Hitting charts, selling out venue after venue, our success has only been another monument to the man who saved my life time and again. That's why the rest of it will be his in some way. Mila not only understands this, but encourages his inclusion in our journey at every step. When the PR company tried to pressure us to distance ourselves from the tragedy after "an appropriate amount of time," she didn't even hesitate before telling them to "fuck off or we'd be 'distancing ourselves' from *them*."

Now, over two years later, I continue to relive his loss as a fresh wound more often than I'm admitting to the others. Only my therapist knows the true depths of how Parker's death still impacts me. But today is about a celebration, so I force the shadows away for another time and place. Maybe I'll let them free later tonight when they can transform into the healing salve of music.

For now, we eat soft pretzels and bust some heads at dodgeball.

∞∞∞

"Dude, no fair!" Reece wails from the other side of the gym.

"Get off the court, loser," I call back, palming a stiff foam ball. Our team has already won the first match. If we take this one, we officially crush the first ever PPY Dodgeball Tournament. My pint-sized teammates are deafening in their support of my strike on Reece.

"You're out!" an excited ten-year-old shrieks, pointing at my bass player.

Reece grunts and slams the ball he's holding on the floor. I give him a taunting look which he returns with some weird gesture that was probably a middle-finger filtered for the presence of children. This only makes me laugh harder.

I scan the few remaining opponents, passing over the kids in favor of my bandmates. Derrick is still in the game, more serious than I've ever seen him. Jay got knocked out in the first ten seconds—probably because he was way more interested in checking out the auditorium sound system than throwing rubber balls around. My theory was confirmed when he skipped off the court and disappeared from the gym before we could even harass him for sucking at sports.

Me? I only have one mode when it comes to physical competition: cutthroat.

I whip my ball at Derrick, who ducks just in time. But the high-pitched yelp he lets out makes the miss totally worth it.

"What was that, dude?" I call over.

He grins back with a valiant arm flex. His throw is way less impressive, and I duck under it easily.

"Jesse, Jesse!" one of my teammates calls over. I turn to the girl and motion for the ball she's preparing to toss me. I catch it and launch an immediate strike back at Derrick. This time he doesn't have a chance and hits the ground like a sack of rocks.

His groan is as fake as his date's orgasm last night. God, that girl made us gag. Sharing a wall with Derrick definitely has its drawbacks.

Without any band members, I skim the spectators for a glimpse of Mila. She refused to play, something about decorum, but I can't accept that. I see her chatting with some important-looking older couple and throw the ball with just enough force to earn me an irritated look.

I shrug innocently, expecting more remote venom. Instead, my girl reaches for the ball and fires it at my knees. The ball smashes into me and bounces away.

"You're out!" Reece calls from the sidelines.

"Mila isn't even playing!" I shout back.

"Aren't I?" she says, slipping off her heels. "You sure about that?" Well, shit.

She marches with frightening determination to the other side of the court. Her game face scares the hell out of me.

"What do we do?" Lacey whispers, sidling up beside me. I crouch to eyelevel, all the while keeping tabs on our few remaining opponents.

"Ms. Mila looks scary, but she has a soft spot for cute kids," I say, extra serious.

Lacey nods gravely, dark brown eyes narrowing on my girlfriend. "I think I could take her, Mr. Jesse," she says.

"You think so?"

She nods.

"Okay. Then this one's yours. I'll distract her. You go in for the kill." I present my fist which she pounds before skating back to position. By her look, I wouldn't want to be Mila Taylor right now.

Mila looks adorable all bent over with her hands on her knees. Butt in the air, expensive suit skirt riding up her thighs, she's the picture of the dimensions I love about her. Hope she doesn't get a tear in those silk stockings. Yeah, that's a lie. That'd be hilarious.

I nod discreetly to Lacey before taking a few steps toward the line of scrimmage.

"Hey, Mila. Why the heck is it called Yorkshire Pudding if it isn't even pudding?"

Her features scrunch into the confused annoyance I was hoping for. Just as she's reaching for a ball to fire at my smart mouth, another one streaks toward her, slamming into her foot.

"Ow!" she cries, bursting into giggles when she finds the culprit. Lacey nearly explodes with pride and rushes over for a high-five. Three minutes later, the other team is depleted, and the few remaining members on mine are exchanging all kinds of disproportionate celebrations.

"Thanks, Mr. Jesse," a small voice squeaks behind me. I turn and kneel to accept the hug of a little boy who can't be more than six.

"You got it, little dude. What's your name?"

"Ben."

"Well, Ben, it's nice to meet you. Did you have fun?"

He nods, long dark curls spilling over his forehead. "Ms. Jean says we can come here lots."

"Yeah? That would be awesome."

"She says you are a famous music-player."

I laugh and shrug. "I don't know. Maybe. I play music, anyway."

His eyes grow huge. "I want to be a music-player too one day."

"Nice! How about we talk to Ms. Jean about the music classes here? Maybe you'd like to take some and learn how to play?"

"Really? A real guitar, even?"

I nod. "A real guitar. Here." I reach in my pocket and pull out a pick. "You'll need this. Be sure to bring it to your first lesson and tell them Jesse sent you."

The little boy's jaw drops as he stares at the object in my hand. Hesitantly, reverently, he collects it from my palm. "I can have this?"

"As long as you promise to use it," I say.

He nods, curls bobbing in approval.

"Tell you what. I have to go get ready to play for the concert tonight. How would you like to sit onstage with us?"

His eyes look ready to pop from his head. "For real?"

I hold out my fist. "For real." He bumps it with a giant smile. "You show them that guitar pick and tell them you're Jesse's friend, okay? Make sure you bring Ms. Jean."

"What about Malik?"

"Is Malik your foster brother?"

He nods.

"Well, then you better bring Malik too."

He shrieks, and before I know it, I'm being tackled by little arms. He pulls away and darts back to the sidelines where a smiling woman who must be "Ms. Jean" waits. It's then that I realize how much my cheeks hurt from grinning.

∞∞∞

We're doing last minute prep before call time when my phone buzzes. I glance down and smile to myself at the name.

"Hey, Luke," I say, tucking the phone against my shoulder so I can lace up my shoes.

"Hey, Jess. I'm not interrupting anything, right?"

"Nah, just about to go onstage."

"Oh, shit. That's right, sorry. Well hey, call me later. I want to hear how the grand opening went."

"Great so far."

"Yeah? That's awesome. Sorry to miss it. I wish we could have been there."

I laugh and switch the phone to the other shoulder. "You've kinda got your hands full, dude. No worries."

"Yeah, but still… Hey, you're still coming tomorrow, right?"

"Wouldn't miss it. We're hopping on the plane right after we finish here."

"Okay, great. Well, I'll let you go. Call me when you have time. Send pictures too."

"For sure."

"And Jess?"

"Yeah?"

"Parker would be so proud of you."

I bite my lip and nod, hoping Luke can sense my response through the phone.

"Call me later," he says, softer, knowing.

I swallow. "Will do."

∞∞∞∞

Ben, Malik, and Ms. Jean sit just offstage in chairs Mila arranged for them. The entire band delivers high-fives and greetings as we pass, and awe bursts off the little cherub faces. Ben holds up his pick, and I give him a thumbs-up.

We continue to the stage where the lights are already signaling that something incredible is about to happen. I'd insisted that the designers and contractors spare no expense when it came to the in-house concert venue. Jay oversaw the AV design himself, and it really is a thing of beauty. I'm honored to be the first to play this room, but I'm also counting the days until I'll be in the audience, watching kids like Ben raise hell up here.

For all the stages I've played throughout my life, there's a special reverence as I step onto this one. The rest of the band seems to sense it as well, and I watch Jay hesitate when he approaches the place where Parker should have been. I smile over at him with a nod. He nods back and settles in.

Drawing in a deep breath, I grip the neck of my guitar and move toward the mic stand. The crowd roars, faces shining, eager and mostly young. I'm out there somewhere, Parker too, along with all the kids like us who didn't have a prayer. But somehow, somehow, we survived—often because of big brothers like Parker Everett who refused to let fate have its way. It may take a lifetime, but I'm going to spend it fighting to be half the man he was. These kids *will* have a prayer and grow up knowing the influence of mentors like Parker. They will be loved, protected, and believed in.

They will know the light that flickers in the darkness.

I stare out over them now, glimpsing the past, anticipating the future. This is it: the start of something that started years ago.

This is your moment, bro. This is all you.

EPILOGUE THREE: LUKE

"Sh—I mean, ouch." I suck on my throbbing finger, while my son critiques my oven skills from his high chair. "Explain to me again why a caterer couldn't do all of this?" I ask Holland who's having way more fun with mushy sweet potatoes and our kid.

"Because it's Parker's first birthday and it needs to be personal. We don't want to be *those people*."

"What people? People who can't cook? Because we are." I duck to avoid the cracker puff that flies at my head. "Careful. I don't want to have to vacuum again too."

Holland snorts a laugh. "Right. Because you're such the domestic genius."

"Hey, I'm the one over here burning my fingers off on these cream puff things."

"They're mini quiches."

"Whatever."

"You volunteered for appetizer duty."

"Better than decoration duty. Those dancing pigs scare the sh—crap out of me. When's Jesse getting here anyway? He's the chef of the group."

She glances at the clock. "Any second, I think. They flew in last night so they're probably sleeping in."

"Daaaaaaaaaa." Tiny arms reach toward me, and I melt into the little puddle of Daddy mush that I become every time that kid looks at me. How such a miracle can come from a mess like me, I'll never understand. Must take after his mother.

I plant a kiss on Holland's head and move to scoop up Parker.

"What are you doing?"

"You look like you need a break," I lie. Holland's eyes narrow, but she has zero resistance to the sight of me losing my shit over our son. The kid's so damn perfect. "We need to work on our song. Don't we, little dude?"

"Daaaaaaa! Daaaaa!"

"See?" I direct to Holland who's crossed her arms in disapproval. Even Parker doesn't buy it. I grab the rag and wipe him down.

"What about the party?"

"Eh, we're good. Besides, your mother is going to re-do everything when she gets here anyway. I'm surprised she didn't stay over so she could start last night."

A smile peeks out on Holland's face. "Well…"

I tuck Little Dude against my shoulder and give his mom a hard look. "What?"

"She *may* have asked to stay over tonight to help after the party. I *may* have said okay."

"Of course you did."

"It's the least we can do for how much she helps with Parker."

"Hey, I'm not complaining. Just don't let her near the studio again. Last time she dusted the mixer and moved all the presets."

Holland bites her lip, trying not laugh. "I promise."

"It's not funny," I say on my way out of the kitchen. It wasn't. I was pissed. Now, several months later, maybe it kinda is.

"Daaaaaaaa?" Parker pads a chubby hand against my cheek.

"I know, dude. We're going."

We make our way through the house, and down the stairs to the finished basement. Parker is already jumping in my arms, struggling against my pace that's not fast enough for his one-year-old schedule. I put him down and let him lead the way to the studio with his zombie-baby strut. Kid's definitely going to be a lead singer like his parents.

He pushes on the glass, adding another handprint to the collection, and I grab his hand before opening the door.

As soon as we're in, he's on the move toward his pint-sized drum kit.

"You ready to work, my man?" I ask, crouching down.

"Daaaaaaaaa!" He climbs up on the little stool-chair and points to his ear protection. I grab the safety muffs and secure them around his head. His grin is everything and matches the one on my phone's lock screen. I barely place the short sticks in his hands before he's banging away on his kit. Yep, the custom four-piece baby set was a shower gift from Casey and Callie. Casey insisted the first NSB kid was going to be a drummer. Parker hasn't figured out the pedal for the kick drum yet, but he loves kicking it.

"Well, hang on. I didn't even tune my guitar yet," I say to no one because my bandmate is long gone in baby-music-land.

I nod my head to his beat as I remove my acoustic from its case. The kid would definitely benefit from some time with a metronome, but for a one-year-old, he's pretty damn solid. Huge blue eyes shine over at me through the banging, and I give him a thumbs-up. I insert my own ears so I can hear my guitar over my son's accompaniment.

Just a man who never knew his plans included you
Just a man who never knew what wild love could do
Just a man with half a world until your smile crowded in
Just a man whose hand will always guide, protect, and hold you.

Parker's giggles join the fray. I can't hear them through the noise and IEMs, but his entire body laughs when he's happy. The first time Holland and I heard that belly-laugh made it official: we were addicted.

Baby boy, your story's just begun
Hold on for the ride, the road's a tragic one
But, baby boy, your story will be legend
Because with the pain comes truth and all that's worth protecting.
Collect the stars, the moon, they're yours for the taking

Baby boy: my heart, my sun, the treasured one
Your time is now, stand tall and sure

There's no mistaking
You're a legend in the making.

Parker smashes away, oblivious to his place in my heart. I smile over, pulling absently at the strings while I enjoy the show. I've lived some epic moments, but spending time in here with this kid and his mother surpasses them all. Funny how with exceptional love comes exceptional fear. I've never cared about myself the way I worry for these two. The way I live and breathe for their happiness and embrace a selflessness that feels as effortless as breathing. Funny that: finding yourself by getting lost in someone else. Here we are, father and son, lost and found in a mini universe that didn't exist until this kid entered our lives. Funny that: life, where so much beauty can come from the ugly, so much joy from the pain. Where we're all legends in the making doing our best to write our stories. Mine is complete and just beginning at the same time. I see that now, how every event, every player has a role in the journey and it's up to us to permit their impact.

I've chosen death, life, and everything in between. I don't know what's next, but I know what's now. And what's now is pretty damn good.

∞∞∞

I try to be a responsible father. Discipline and all that crap, but I'm a total pushover when it comes to studio time. Parker calls the shots inside this room, so by the time he finishes his imaginary set, our house is much fuller when we emerge from the basement.

"Uhhhhhhhhh!" Parker twists from my arms, frantic to reach the young man who looks just as excited to see him.

"Dude! Where you been?" Jesse says, kneeling down and opening his arms for his surrogate nephew. Parker waddles at full speed and wraps his arms around Jesse's neck.

"Well, Uncle Jesse was late so we were killing time in the studio," I say, quirking a smile.

He rolls his eyes. "I'm not late. Party doesn't even start for another hour, right?"

"He needs you to finish the appetizers!" Holland calls from the kitchen.

Jesse laughs and lifts Parker with him. Balancing him on his hip, he makes his way toward the kitchen. "I thought I'd get to be on baby duty today," he says. "We need some uncle time. Right, my man?" Jesse presents his fist which Parker acknowledges with a sloppy grin.

Mila smirks and pops one of the mini quiches in her mouth. Her face scrunches with disapproval of my culinary skills. "What's this supposed to be again?" She doesn't exactly spit it out, but she might as well at this point.

Jesse chuckles and joins her at the island. He pokes a finger from his free hand at one of my creations. "You're lucky your mommy and daddy can afford to hire professionals," he mutters to my son.

"Hey, I heard that," Holland says.

Jesse shrugs. "Just telling it like it is. My nephew is not going to grow up eating"—he shudders—"whatever this is. Why didn't you bring in a caterer?"

"Holland wants to keep it low-key."

"Right," he says with a smirk. "Well, you've accomplished that."

"Please, Jess?" Holland even bats her big blue eyes at him. Damn, she's desperate.

He shakes his head, tucks his hair behind his ear, and plops Parker on the counter. He leans down until they're eye-level. "Okay, my man. Looks like your mommy and daddy need Uncle Jesse right now. But you better save time for me later, got it?"

"Uhhhhhhhhhhh!"

Jesse presses his fingertips into Parker's tummy, eliciting a shriek that has us all laughing. He picks him up again and lowers him to the floor. "Later, dude." He presents his fist once more—and gets the same sloppy grin as before. "One day we'll get this down," he says, grabbing Parker's little fist and tapping it to his.

Jesse straightens as Parker takes off toward the living room.

"Leave it with me!" Mila says, following after him.

Holland and I turn back to Jesse who's washing his hands at the sink.

"So what am I making?" he calls back.

∞∞∞

Holland's family shows up next of course. Her parents, sisters, and even Shandor, Sylvie's boyfriend and Holland's lead guitar player all enter loud, enthusiastic, and bearing obscene amounts of gifts. We're only missing Hannah who's coming later with Wes. For the record, I had to talk Holland out of turning Parker's first birthday party into an engagement party for her sister. I swear she was probably more excited than Hannah about their news.

Mila doesn't stand a chance with the baby once Grandma and Pappy descend on the scene. Parker does his usual display of irresistible baby charm to manipulate all the adults into his personal entourage. You don't know power until you've seen what idiocy a one-year-old can elicit from seasoned grownups.

Confident that the birthday boy is being properly smothered with supervision, I check on Jesse in the kitchen. He's recruited help from Sylvie and one of Holland's friends who's very clearly developed a crush on our chef.

"How's it going in here?" I ask.

"Fine," Jesse says, spooning delicious-smelling sauce into a bowl. "You owe me some serious baby time for this. Like exclusive one-on-one Uncle Jesse studio time."

"Yeah, yeah." I lean over the bowl. Damn, that smells heavenly. I grab a spoon and yep. Oh my god.

"It's a sweet chili sauce for the chicken skewers. Is it okay?"

"It's amazing, man."

Jesse nods. "Good. Hey, can I send Pappy Drake out to the grill?"

"You trust him with your food?"

"I had his steak at that cookout over the summer. He's legit."

I nod. "You got it. Let me know if you need anything else."

Jesse's already moving on to the next project, barking orders at his sous chefs like he's paying them exorbitant salaries. In reality, he's mostly showing them how to hold a knife and peel shit.

I give Holland's father his assignment and answer the door for more guests. And by guests, I mean crowds. Geez, did Holland invite the entire city? Toronto is a big place. I'm surprised Callie and Casey aren't here yet, until I remember they were flying in from Houston this morning. It's been a month since I last saw Callie. Way too long, but our schedules have been a nightmare lately. I check my phone for an update from either of them, but nothing yet.

"You okay?" Holland asks, snaking her arms around my waist. I pull her against me and kiss her.

"Fine. Just worried about Cal and Case."

"Still haven't heard anything?"

I shake my head.

"What time was their flight supposed to get in?"

"Not sure."

"That's not like Callie."

"I know. That's why I'm concerned."

"Well, I haven't seen anything in the news about a fiery plane crash or alien abductions…"

We exchange a look. She's trying to keep a straight face.

"That's not funny," I say, smiling anyway.

"I know." She leans her head on my shoulder. "How's the song coming?"

"Parker's?"

I feel her nod.

"Good. Almost finished. Want to hear it?"

She squeezes harder, pressing straight through to my heart. "Yes. But not right now. Too many witnesses to see me become a blubbering mess."

I smile and kiss her hair, unable to believe this is my life. An orphan enjoying a house packed with family? A second-chance survivor learning to live and nurture new life? Who would have thought a throwaway kid from South Africa would end up in a Kingdom of Promise? Who would have thought… my dad, probably. Callie. Casey. Holland. So many others who had no business believing in me when I'd given up on myself. Yes, maybe we're all at risk of becoming blubbering messes when the time is right.

I clear my throat. Blink some moisture from my eyes. "Same, babe. Same."

Epilogue Four: Callie

"Did you tell Luke we'll be late?"

Casey slides his hand over and secures it on my bouncing knee.

"No. It's better he gets nervous."

"That's mean."

"That's half the fun of pranks. You think I wasn't scared every time those hotel workers knocked with another gift from Marty Heilman? Or when actual Roman dancers came waltzing in to our reception?"

A smile slips over my lips. My husband is the most easygoing man I know. The sight of him so riled the week of our wedding still haunts me. Marty Heilman became the symbol of the mess of that week, and that's the *only* reason I've allowed revenge. Plus kittens. Kittens are freaking cute.

They're mewing in the back of the rental car now, and I peek for another look.

"We're not keeping one," Casey warns.

"But they're so adorable! Those widdle tiny faces." I smoosh mine to match theirs as if we'll connect on a deeper level. I swear it works. "Luke is going to kill you, you know," I direct to the other human in the car.

Casey doesn't seem remotely bothered by that. "He loves animals."

"Right. Well, I still feel like this is disproportionate punishment. Once Parker sees these, they're locked in."

"That's the plan."

Gosh that smile. Still melts me into useless puddles. My man has been gaining lots of attention lately with the rise of Penchant for Red and NSB's return to superstardom. So many fangirls turning their bedroom fantasies into action plans. On the road, online, you'd think he was a porn star, not a musician, the way they ogle him. Casey takes it in stride like everything else, but it still gets under my skin. One blog called him Sex-With-A-Stick, in what I'm guessing was their bid for the worst pun of the year. Casey thought it was funny. I thought we should sue for the cheese-factor alone. It's even worse for Luke, but the guys mostly ignore it.

I glance over at him now and watch his fingers tap unconscious beats on the steering wheel. Even in silence, there's music in his head. Always music. It's my hand reaching across the seat this time and settling on his thigh. He looks over, surprised.

"Whoa. What's this?"

I shrug. "Just thinking."

"About how hot I am?" His favorite line. But today…

"Maybe."

I get the grin I'd been hoping for, and maybe if not for Parker and the kittens I'd tell him to pull over right here right now. I swear I've been hornier since I found out. That can't be normal, right? Then again other pregnant women aren't married to Casey Barrett. I think the researchers probably don't account for that variable in their studies.

I haven't told him yet. They were on the road, and I wanted to do it in person, and then he just got back and we had to get on the plane and it was so chaotic, and the other passengers, and the running around, and now we're here. My knee starts bouncing again. I want to tell him so badly, but I also don't want to crash our car.

Besides, only three tests verified it. Maybe I should take a fourth just to be sure?

I study the profile of the future father of my child. Perhaps it's hormones, but the pressure builds in my chest. If he's half the father he is as a husband, our kid will be the luckiest squirt on the planet. And I know he'll be more than I can imagine. That's Casey. Strong, fearless, funny, and ridiculously talented. The world needs plenty more tiny versions of him running around. Maybe a few of me too.

"What's so funny?" he asks.

My smile grows despite my attempts to clamp it down with my teeth. Who am I kidding? I can't wait. "Can you pull over in that lot quick?"

"Uh sure. You need to pee?"

I shake my head, still trying not to smile.

"Um… okay." Poor guy is crazy confused. He parks the car by a Tim Horton's, and the pregnant part of my brain is already planning a trip inside for a bagel or donut. Maybe one of those wraps. When do they start serving lunch?

"What's going on?" he asks, turning to me.

"Nothing, just. Before we go to the party I wanted to tell you something."

He lifts a brow, clearly concerned. I'm still trying not to grin like an idiot.

"Which is?" he encourages when I still don't speak.

I clear my throat, my pulse racing. "Well, I thought you should know before we see Luke's baby that if all goes well, we'll be having our own next year."

My teeth press into my lip, fists clenched as I wait. Casey's eyes, usually bright with humor, are freaking enormous with… all the things. My gosh. I feel a giggle bubbling in my stomach.

"Waaaait…" He blinks. Shakes his head. Blinks again. "Waaaait… No…"

I nod, tears pricking the corners of my eyes. "I found out two days ago when you were in Las Vegas, but I wanted to tell you in person."

Still no words from my beloved. Lots of blinking and goofy grinning though. Then suddenly, "Yes! Yes, yes, yes!" He pumps his fist like he just won the mother of all Grammys, and before I know it, I'm being dragged across the console to the driver's side of the car.

"You're squishing me," I laugh.

"Oh my god. I'm sorry!" He pushes me back, patting my head awkwardly. "Did I hurt the baby? Shit! I'm so sorry, I'm just…"

"Dork," I say, climbing back over the console to straddle his lap.

His smile… I just can't. I take his face in my hands and kiss him. Gently at first, then more and more and more because it's not enough, and now I need to draw in love for two.

"You're going to be a father, Casey Barrett," I whisper. "You're going to be an amazing father."

Our gazes lock as I trace his smile with my finger.

"Damn. Doesn't that scare the hell out of you?" he murmurs.

"Heck, yeah." I brush my lips against his again. "But there's no one I'd rather figure it out with than you."

His smile returns. "I mean, Luke and Holland figured it out."

"Exactly."

The kittens seem just as excited about the news, and maybe I take another peek back.

"Wait…" Casey says, eyes narrowing. "The timing… This wasn't some ploy to let you keep a kitten?"

It's my turn to grin. I shrug and let the giggle out when he tickles my side.

"Seriously?" he asks once we've calmed back into each other's arms. "We're actually going to have a baby?"

"We're having a baby." It sounds so incredible. So terrifying. So perfect. Well, almost.

My attention flickers to the back of the car. "And a kitten."

∞∞∞

We pull up to the house, small by Texas standards but huge for the Greater Toronto Area. Luke and Holland settled just a few blocks from her parents shortly before Parker was born. Good for the Drake family, terrible for us. Then again, we're always traveling anyway. They keep a guestroom just for us, and I'm giddy with the thought that soon they'll need to add a bassinet. Maybe we could just use Parker's? I'm already picturing cousins growing up together, because let's be honest, we're as related at this point as anyone can be without technical definitions.

I glance at Casey, who still seems to be working on the task of breathing like a normal person.

"You know, you're going to have to play it much cooler before we go in there," I warn. "We can't tell anyone yet. Not for a few weeks."

He looks downright tortured by this.

"Maybe just Luke and Holland?" Is he begging? So cute.

"Hmm…"

"Come on, Cal. How can we not tell Luke?"

"I don't know…"

Currency. I know what I want. How much is it worth to him?

A scowl spreads over his face. "Fine. You can keep a kitten."

"Promise?" I ask, clasping my hands.

"Promise."

"The little black one."

"Sure."

"And her name will be Frankie."

"Whatever."

I clap again, already picturing all the little beds and towers and toys she'll have.

"She doesn't sleep with us," he adds.

I laugh at the absurd statement but let it go. I'll set him straight later. For now, our focus is wrecking our best friend's happy day.

"Three kittens is a lot," Casey says, glancing back at our stash.

"Well, only two now. You having second thoughts?"

"Hell no."

The trunk is packed with cat supplies (we're not total jerks), but we thought it would be more effective to present Parker's fluffy birthday presents unadorned. We'll grab that stuff once the excitement and overwhelming gratitude for our generosity has run its course.

"So how are we doing this? You sticking them in your purse?" Casey asks.

"It's not a purse. It's meant to carry small animals."

"So... a purse."

"A pet carrier."

"A pet purse."

"Fine."

Compromise. That's how marriage works.

"So let's shove those things in the pet purse..."

"There is no shoving when it comes to kittens!"

He rolls his eyes. "You know what I mean."

"And there will be no shoving Frankie—ever."

"Okay, poor word choice. I would never hurt an animal. I'm the one who rescued your spider from the hotel, remember?"

True. I soften a bit. Although he always looks kind of guilty when he talks about that spider for some reason.

"You ready?" he asks.

I nod and exit the car to move to the back with the large pet carrier. The kittens are legit the cutest things ever as I transfer them to my "pet purse." Their little squeaks and rumbles and paws. Oh my gosh. I can't.

Casey is shaking his head, unimpressed when I finally rejoin human world.

"Don't lie. You think they're adorable too."

All three were rescues from a shelter and have a clean bill of health from a local vet. Yes, we researched that for them also. The place is just a few blocks away and has very flexible hours. I doubt Luke and the guys did this much legwork with their pranks. Then again, how hard is it to find and book an Ancient Roman dance troupe? There's a question I never thought I'd have to consider.

"Alright. I'm ready. And you are too, right, little ones?" My voice gets all pitchy when I talk to animals. Casey makes fun of me, but I tell him he has the same expression when he's looking at band equipment. He got more excited about his new kick pedal last week than I've ever been over anything.

We make our way toward the front entrance, and I do my best to act like my classy, well-disguised pet purse doesn't have kittens inside. Casey rings the bell and gets crushed into a hug.

"Hey, man," Luke says. He's so relieved that I almost feel badly. He will definitely not be in a few minutes. "Callie."

I adjust the purse so I can go in for a hug.

"Been too long," he says quietly, and I squeeze him harder.

"Definitely." We talk all the time but it's not the same as seeing someone's smile and squeezing affection out of them. I pull back and study his face. He looks younger than when we met. The lines in his face have relaxed, and there's a light that warms my heart. I always sensed how special he was, that beneath the layers of pain was a man anyone would be honored to encounter. It's deeply satisfying to be right. To see the evidence harden into fact.

"Well, come in. We were worried when we hadn't heard from you," he says, stepping back so we can enter.

"Sorry, man. We had some stops to make on the way."

"Yeah?" he says.

Casey doesn't elaborate, and I see the questions forming in Luke's head. He knows us too well not to be suspicious.

"Where's the birthday boy?" I ask before we blow our cover entirely. Plus, it's getting hard to disguise the fact that my "purse" keeps moving on its own. At least the house is so loud that we can't hear the kitten chirps.

"With Holland's mom, I think. This way."

Casey and I exchange a quick smile before following Luke through the house toward the main family room. It's so sleek and clean and devoid of cat fur.

We're not at all surprised to see Parker surrounded by fawning adults. The kid owns the room wherever he goes. He's got his dad's expressive eyes and his mom's beautiful smile. Plus a mop of soft curls that's not even fair.

"Yo, Park!" Casey shouts through the ruckus. The room quiets and the little guy searches for the cause. When his gaze lands on us, that devastating baby smile turns kitten-cute into a distant memory.

"Uhhhhhh!" he screeches, lurching toward us.

"That's right, my man. Uncle Casey and Auntie Callie are here to spoil you rotten."

"You already have," Holland mutters behind us. Casey flashes her a grin, and I'm squirming with excitement. This couldn't be more perfect. Everyone's here. Everyone's quiet. Parker is already fired up.

"We brought you a special present," I say, bending down.

I don't have to see our hosts' faces to know their reactions. Casey's glee reflects them perfectly.

I gently place my purse on the carpet, and Parker leans over to inspect, eyes wide.

"These are from your Daddy's friend Marty Heilman."

Parker starts clap-dancing, and I can't resist a look back. Luke is as pale as I've ever seen him. Holland just looks stunned into silent horror. I open the purse and flinch at the shriek.

Parker already has his hands near the opening, and I grab them. "Just a second, little man."

I pull out a kitten, loving the look on the baby's face. He's not even clapping anymore. All his energy must be in that grin. "See? We pet gently." I take his hand and run it over the furry back of the kitten. His squeal is priceless. Casey looks triumphant and crouches to take the kitten so I can grab the other.

"Two?" Luke chokes out behind us.

Parker bounces in place, clapping and squealing.

"Gentle," I remind him, guiding his hand over the other kitten. He looks past my shoulder and points at his parents, then back at the kitten. So much pointing. Casey and I snicker.

By Luke's glare when he joins us on the floor, our plan worked beautifully. "You two are—"

"You mean, Marty?" Casey interrupts, raising a brow. He even shrugs to emphasize his innocent bystander status in all of this.

I actually see the moment when Luke swallows his irritation and forces a smile for his son. Yep, they're so keeping these fur-balls. There's nothing funnier, cuter, and hotter, than watching grown men cave to tiny-human dimples.

"Wow, *Marty*," he mutters. "Thanks so much."

Thing is, the only thing more heart-melting than a handful of kittens is Luke's kid. Luke's kid with a kitten? Yeah, even Holland's frown has turned upside down into mild appreciation. Parker? Still pointing and flashing killer dimples.

"Guess we'll be heading out to the pet store," Luke says, scooping one of the kittens from the floor. Wait, is that a smile? He's such a softy.

My own grin is so huge it's starting to get painful.

"We brought supplies. Don't worry," I say.

"Really?"

"Of course. We'll go grab them from the car."

Luke nods and puts the kitten back on the carpet. "I'll help. You good with Parker and the… cats?" he directs to Holland.

She seems eager to get rid of us so she can cuddle some kittens herself. "Fine." We are waved away with one hand while the other locks in with babies and kittens.

Out at the car, Casey pops the trunk and Luke lets out a low whistle. "Wow. You weren't kidding."

"Should be everything you need," I say. "Litterbox and supplies, food, scoop, toys, cat beds, cat tree. Oh and that's for cleaning stains out of your carpet." I add a smile to that.

"Great, thanks." He reaches for the box of litter. "You guys staying over tonight?"

"We're planning on it if it's still okay," Casey says.

"Of course. We'd love that. Just to warn you, the mother-in-law is staying too, apparently."

"That's fine. She can have our room if she wants."

Luke almost looks offended. "No way. We keep that one for you. It's got all your crap in it anyway. She can have the den. She'll probably camp out in Parker's room anyway."

"Okay, that works," Casey says.

"Oh hey," I interject. "Would you mind if we added a bassinet to our room for next year's visits?"

Luke nods. "Sure. In fact I can just set up Park... wait..."

I grin. Casey beams. Luke drops a box of litter on the driveway.

"Are you... No... You're...?"

His face, oh my gosh. Wish I had my camera.

"Think Parker would mind growing up with a virtual cousin?" I ask. It's the last words out of my mouth before I'm crushed in a giant Luke Craven hug. I squeeze him back, laughing as he swings me around.

"Careful with her!" Casey shouts.

Instead, Luke grabs my husband and pulls him into the huddle.

"This is the best news ever. I'm..." Are those tears in his eyes? Maybe they're just reflections through my own. I can't help wrapping my arms around them again. This moment is everything. This bond that no one and nothing could break no matter how hard life tried. I'm beyond proud of Luke, of myself, of Casey. I used to picture myself as a hammer, responsible for breaking the glass of Luke's lying mirror. Now, I see I'm more than that. We all are. We don't just break down the lies, but reflect back the truth. We're mirrors too. And torches. And explosive supernovas capable of rocking fate to its core. How else do you explain how one small act, the tiniest choice, can change the world?

We are human, and we are miracles.

EXPLORE THE NSB SERIES

It started with a chair. It ended in legend. Experience the entire NSB Series from the beginnings.

Continue reading for more on each book and the original lyrics that tell their own stories.

NIGHT SHIFTS BLACK

NSB #1 explores Callie, Luke, and Casey's stories.

Synopsis:

His name is Luke. But nobody knows that. He was an iconic musician before he gave up music. But nobody knows that either. They also don't know he's twenty-seven, that he used to have an infectious laugh, and that he's way too young to be widowed. They certainly don't know the rest of his tragic story. All they know is that he comes into their café at the same time every morning and stares at the same chair at the same table. They know he's strange. They know he interrupts their breakfast with a cold blast of air as he hovers in the doorway, mustering the courage to confront a piece of furniture.

No one asks why. No one cares. He's fine with that. He's done with life. This isn't even his story anymore. It's actually Callie's, the young writer who sat in his chair one day.

"Greetings from the Inside"
(Also a recorded song.)

Mirror, mirror what do you see
When you were looking back at me

Mirror, mirror what are you thinking
I see those staring eyes

Mirror, mirror what are you saying
It's always something I believe

Mirror, mirror you're a liar
So why do you own me?

Hello! Hello! Greetings from the inside
Hello! Hello! Framed in all your lies
Hello! Hello! How you love to see me cry
Always so unkind

Mirror, mirror you're shattering
There's more than meets the eye with me
Mirror, mirror you're a liar
So why do you own me?

Hello! Hello! Greetings from the inside
Hello! Hello! Framed in all your lies
Hello! Hello! How you love to see me cry
Always so unkind

Hello. Hello. Greetings from the inside.
Hello. Hello. Framed in all your lies.

Hello! Hello! Greetings from the inside
Hello! Hello! Framed in all your lies.
Hello! Hello! How you live to see me cry
Always so…

"Stay"

How was I supposed to know your smile was only a distraction?
How am I supposed to feel, stuck in veiled conversation?
Because you never let me in, now I have to watch you drowning.
Quiet suffering speak!

I'll stay here, don't look down.
There's nothing waiting for you on the ground.
You're stronger than you're feeling now.
I'll stay here.
I'll stay.

How was I supposed to know you wore silence like some worn out
    fashion?
How are you supposed to heal, so afraid of our reaction?
Because you have to let me in, please stop all of this pretending.
Oh quiet suffering speak!

Quiet suffering, I hear it. Deafening.
Quiet suffering, I feel it. Pounding.
Stop these games, you don't need it. They're maddening.
Quiet suffering, I don't believe it. I'm waiting.

I'll stay here, don't look down.
There's nothing waiting for you on the ground.
You're stronger than you're feeling now.
I'll stay.

"Unspoken"

I could have told you everything would be alright.
I could have told you it gets easier the harder you try.
But I couldn't lie to you, even though I'd die for you.
And I could have told you instead of just holding you.

But what could I say that my eyes haven't already said?
And what words could heal the wounds that bleed like this?
How many tears will it take to drown away the pain?
I don't know, but I can hold you.

And I could have taken you far away from here.
But where would that leave you? It'd be the same even there.
I won't hide you, even though I'd like to.
And I could have spoken instead of just loving you.

But what could I say that my eyes haven't already said?
And what words can heal the wounds that break us?
How many tears will it take to drown away the pain?
I don't know, but I can hold you. I can love you.
I can hold you.

"I'm Yours"

They say I'm a rock star, baby
But that's just what they made me
Ignore my wall of Grammys, right now I'm only yours.

I'm a superstar or pathetic cover, it's all in your power, lover
You're everything I need to know, let me be yours

I'm no titan, hon, a liar, maybe
I'm no one else you need to know
You unravel my maze, the light in my haze
You're everything I need to know

You may drive me crazy
But when I'm with you I'm just Casey, and that's how I know,
that's all I need to know,
I'm yours

"Perfect Day"

It's a perfect day for candlelight, let it cast its shadow.
It's a perfect day for apathy.
It's a perfect day for tragedy, eclipsed by a moment in time.
It's a perfect day, why not today?

It's a perfect day, don't wait up for a tearful goodbye.
It's a perfect day for illusion.
It's a perfect day for solace, I'll make this easy on you.
Don't you worry, it's a perfect day, why not today?

Can you hear me, screaming some lie, disguising the truth
Can you see me, bleeding, I'm unraveling
Shattering
Do you remember what you told me, 'Everything has its place and
   time?'
Well, that's fine, you can look away, you're just proving it's the
   perfect day.

"Laughing Stock"

It's not funny how far you've strayed, I'll say it one time
I can tell by your smile you know I'm right, still you hide behind
    the lie.
It's not funny how far you've strayed, I'll say it this time.
I can tell by your eyes you know what I mean, still you find a
    reason to fight, but you'll never cry.

How can you believe it's easier to be alone than feel loved?
You fear the embrace of a friend, yet welcome your enemies' hands
    as they beat down.
You listen for proof that no one understands you, but we do
And it's killing me.

It's not funny to see how well you ignore the signs.
By the pain in your eyes I can see you're fading.
Still you try, you're losing the fight.

You're no better for falling apart
Being alone won't make you stronger
You'll fall harder the more space you put between us
But I'll catch you, oh I'll catch you.

How can you believe it's easier to feel alone than feel loved?
You fear the embrace of a friend, yet welcome your enemies' hands
    as they beat down.
You listen for proof that no one understands you, but I do
And it's killing me. It's killing me!

It's not funny how far you've strayed, just listen this one time
Look in my eyes and see how I love you.

"Too Late"

Isn't it obvious our feelings fade away
Isn't it obvious it's too late to make a change
So I wait for the innocent moment of truth
You want a sign, demanding your proof

It's too late for answers
Too late for questions
Too late for telling lies
Too late for pleading
Too late for reason
You know it's time, oh it's time

Isn't it obvious amidst our cold embrace
Isn't it obvious there's too much to erase
And you wait for the shadow of a memory
Here's your sign, you barely saw me leave

A picture's worth a thousand words
Let's leave them as memories…

Tracing Holland

NSB #2 explores Luke, Holland, Wes, Jesse, Callie, and Casey's stories.

Synopsis:

Second chances are hard enough when you deserve them. Then there are the ones you don't.

Callie asked if I was ready. And that's the question, isn't it? Ready for what? The spotlight? The music? Or ready for life. Ready to face the reality that what I was is going to attack the very fabric of who I am now. No one knows I'm a different person. Well, no one except the two most important people in my life, which is why there's a remote chance I might actually pull off the comeback I never saw coming.

Then again, that was before Holland Drake crashed into my life. I didn't ask for her. Heaven knows she didn't ask for me. But sometimes it's not about what makes sense; it's about accepting that not everything will. It's learning you have a choice when it feels like you don't. It's believing even the worst past can still have a future.

And sometimes it's none of that. Sometimes it's survival. A blind fight through the pain as you cling to any shred of hope you can find. And it's those moments, those desperate pleas into the darkness for a flicker of light, when you have no choice but to confront the blessing that often feels like a curse:

You're still alive. You're still significant.

You're once again Luke Craven, frontman for Night Shifts Black.

"Metamorphosis"

Crawl in, crawl out
Terrified but moving now
Claw up, slide down
There's no going back, can't go back

Break down, break out
Break down, break out

Brand new day feast on the dark
Shuttered light, reluctant spark
Growing dawn and setting sun
Fight song of the desperate one.

Cocoon shredding
Past, heading straight for the wall
No more regretting, just breathing
Underwater

Too late to choose, too far to fall
Nowhere to go but on
No more excuses, no denial
No holding on to lost time

Break out, I'm breaking out

Brand new day release the dark
A new light, the smallest spark
Growing dawn and setting sun

Fight song of the desperate one.

Break it down, break it
Breaking out, just break it, break it

"Acrobat"

Flying high as you watch me fall.
Twisting in your beautiful lies, bravo.
Hats off to your elegant show.
Take a bow, my acrobat.
You've won the crowd, it's yours now, sweet acrobat.

"Perfect Storm"

You and me, babe, a tidal wave I never saw coming.
You and me, and that hurricane we can't outrun.
It shouldn't have been, but there's no fight against the wind.
It all blew in, too fast, too hard, the Perfect Storm.

You and me, babe, still afraid but locked into fate.
You and me, losing all the reasons to run.
Oh sweet ecstasy of defeat, forgive me now.
It all blew in, too hard, too fast, the Perfect Storm.

And I will fight through the waves
To get to you, to get to you
And I will scream through the dark
Against the lies, against the lies that overtake me.

"The Wanderer"

Guide me toward the light, I swear I'll follow.
Forgive me for the man I am.
Fight the hollow ghost I carry.
I've learned to hide the tears,
Though they still break me.

Search for me, the broken wanderer
Find me, deep within my own void
Save me, from my burning lies
Don't believe what I am

I'm a fallen angel,
The disease you can't understand
I'm the reason you've lost faith, your sin
But I'm a liar, don't believe me, please don't believe me

Guide me toward the light, I swear I'll follow
Hold me til the hollowness is gone
These tears mean nothing in the darkness
Don't believe what I am.
I need you to believe when I can't
That I'm more, more than I am.

"Nowhere Man"

I'm Nowhere Man in nowhere spaces
Everywhere a thousand faces, places spill from beneath the
wreckage
Oh it's over now
Oh oh it's over

I'm Forgotten Man in endless races
Chasing air with futile paces, traces of the craft that made us
Oh it's over now
Oh oh it's over

You say you see me, but it's just my shadow
I'm not waiting, just fading past the time you remember
I'm Forgotten Man, Nowhere Man
Light a candle before I'm gone.

I'll run this race, it's still my anthem
Past the shame, the pain is where I fight now
I'm a blaze, a fire, a final hour
Oh it's not over
Oh oh it's not
It's never over

VIPER

NSB #3 explores Wes, Holland, and Luke's stories.

Synopsis:

It's not easy being the bad guy.

Yeah, that's a lie. It's pretty damn simple. You act and you own it. You sell your soul to protect those you love and screw the rest.

It's the restraint that's hard. The demons that poke at your trigger, burn in your gut—just waiting for a second of freedom to unleash the fire in your soul.

Call me a villain. Call me whatever helps you sleep at night and feel good about the black and white of love. But watch your back because I don't care. Until I do.

And then I implode.

"Unraveling"

Fire of mine, ashes of regret
Redeem the manic truth.
Proving scars in vain effect
With no doubts left to lose.

Seven scars from timid youth—six I've left undone.
Since here I am unraveling
And it only took the one.

"Sweetest Death"

Hell's fire and Hades' desire, have nothing on you, babe.
Nothing on you.

Reigning kings tossed worthless rings with less hunger than my
desperate plunder for your treasure.
Better, you tell me no, and save my soul, before your charm,
disarms all that I am.

Breathe my last, through your lungs.
The sweetest death.

"Session in Progress"

Session in progress
The hardest journey we take
Raise a glass to the past, it's the future we break

If all goes well or damns you to hell, it's your story to own
So tell if you dare, to care about your mess, in progress.

"Viper Rising"

Coil of strength wound tight
to hide
to lie
to wither and writhe
In its prison it cries, 'Coil of rage!'

Dirty secrets revealed
The bed
I made
Was never the place
To trap this broken soul, It's over!

Stand back, you're gonna want to stand back

I'm breaking free to strike
Fangs bared, spring out, out
Of hell, don't tell
Me what I am
I'm not, not your pet
I'm your hidden regret
So hear me, you should fucking fear me!
As I rise

"Whiskey Theater"

Her darkness is mine
Desperate to hide,
In the lie of
Breathing hard.
Igniting skin, she sins in the betrayal of lust
She just needs a sign that she's alive and
Free to fly.

"Bloody Heart"

Bloodshot eyes scratch through the veil and find you, find you
Truth locked beyond my reach
You flood in, addictive fangs, sink deep
So deep I bled
For you,
Fled, for you
Chased the moon, I died and came back for you

Wrapped in you
Trapped trapped, before I knew
How to survive the loss
When you find me too, those hidden parts
I blocked, beyond your reach

Your perfection is
My rejection, burns
Hot through the bloody heart you own
Until the beat, beat, beat
Stops.

LIMELIGHT

NSB #4 explores Jesse and Luke's stories.

Synopsis:

I'm unpredictable.
A genius, an underachiever.
I'm the song, the voice, the passion, the pain.
I am failure.
I do music because it's what I am, but sometimes that's not
enough.
A slave to my nature, I wait for it to show mercy and drop a
gift in my lap.
Because the music chose me.
I'm its victim not its gift.

She destroyed my career.
Ruined my life.
Pushed me from the shadows and exposed my lies.
She's the fire that destroys lesser men,
and now her flames are aimed at me.
She loves to watch me burn,
but the part we never saw coming?

Sometimes it takes a fire to ignite a spark
And slay the darkness.

"Nothing I Want'

Stop beggin' for the hunt, babe. You've got nothing I want. Hey—
Keep checkin' for clues, cuz I refuse your bait.

Just wait. Your games were a mistake. Hey—
Maybe your lies work on other guys but this one's checking out.
You've got nothing I want.
Nothing, no, no, nothing I want.

"Jonas"

*Little light of mine. Flicker, flicker burn, until I learn to slay the
ghost of hope, the fucking joke you've made of me.*

*Little friend of mine. Don't be kind when you grind our past into
lasting crimes that might just be the end of me.*

Traitor. Fool me once.
Traitor. Fool me twice.
That knife you hold is so damn pretty.
How's it look in my back? Hey hey

My reaction time is lacking
No backtracking now that you've got me on the prowl
Hey hey
I'm looking at you, traitor, faker, promise-breaker,
Re-arranger of the lies we've tried to bury
Hey hey
I'm looking at you, pretender, mender, truth-blender
Defender of the game I thought we ended
Yeah, yeah, I'm looking at you

"Candlelight"

Another night in the candlelight
Not bright enough to see my scars, just enough to
Fight, Fight
Burn out
Fade out
Cry out against demon screams
Broken dreams
All that keeps me breathing in the dark
Hold tight tight
Just a spark.
Another night.
It'll be all right.
in the candlelight.

AN NSB WEDDING 298

"Agitator"

Overrated, garage-band wasted, talent-jaded
They said

Destined for rejection, binding imperfections, nothing but
objections
They said, they said

Attractive fraud, where's your army now to defend the legend that
only exists in
Could have beens
Would have beens
Should have been vapors assaulted by the wind

Attractive fraud, where's your army now?

Could have been,
Would have been,
Should, should, should have been
Too hazy for a spotlight
They said

Couldn't be
Shouldn't be
Would, would, wouldn't be if not for helping hands that cower
under streetlights

You're special she said
A fucking god beneath the fraud she said

Could be
Should be
Won't be
Unless she collects
the lies she tells

I'm no god, just a piece of hell
Here to tell you how it is

That I could be, should be.
And I will.

"Philadelphia"

Rewind back to the start
And your heart would still be too big for me
Love is a game
For some a lie
For you an epic tie that bound you
To the one who cries
When the lights go out
When the chill seeps down
Through cracks you always mended

Arms that braved the fiercest storms
Swarmed, warmed a broken boy
Who never had a chance
To dance with fate
Who lived afraid of himself

That's love in a city of demons
A pity they never saw you coming

Rewind back to the day
A superhero roared,
"It's okay
To fly, to dream, to spread broken wings
To scale a mountain in spite of it all."

"Brother," he said.
"I'll catch you when you fall."

An NSB Wedding

NSB #5 conclude's the series with Casey and Callie's stories (along with the rest of the NSB gang).

Synopsis:

They say every happily ever after needs a wedding. Heaven knows after the hell we've survived, we deserve the mother of all HEAs. All the pieces are in place. All the players, assembled. The Wedding of the Century is locked and loaded.

Too bad nothing's fair in love, rock, and wedding planning. Too bad sometimes epic happiness requires an epic fail. Guess we should have seen it coming.

Did we expect anything less from AN NSB WEDDING?

"Can It Be Me?"

Words and Music by Jon Meckes
Used with permission

(Also a recorded song)

I can only dream of ending all the waiting
Praying that I'll see you again
Traveling the world I've seen so many others
But I can't keep from thinking of you

But I still walk alone
Should I just move along

Since I'm far away do you look for someone closer
Maybe one to sweep you away
Someone who can hold you
Like I've always wanted to
Oh how I wish that I was there

But I still walk alone
Should I just move along
Only time will tell
If I can be the one inside your dreams
Can it be me?

I don't mean to scare you
I just need to hear you
Tell me that there's nothing for me to fear

But I still walk alone

Should I just move along
Only time will tell
If I can be the one inside your dreams
Can it be me?

I have so many questions
That need to stay unanswered
How will I know the time is right

But I still walk alone
Should I just move along
Only time will tell
If I can be the one inside your dreams
Can it be me?

I hate to have suspicions
It's hard when there's a distance
Like the one that's keeping us apart
So if you feel the same way
Come on out and tell me
I would love to only wait for you.

"Always"
Words and music by Jon Meckes
Used with permission

(Also a recorded song)

It's time to tell you how I feel
I know you've been waiting
I know you've been wondering when

It's time to let go of the past
There's nothing but heartache
Nothing worth keeping now

I want to give you the world
And all that I have
I want to make you my baby
To have and to hold
I want to give you my word
I'll never let go
I'll never let go

I, I won't give you up
Cause I don't want to live without you by my side
Forevermore I want you always
As long as I'm alive
I'll have you 'til the end of time
I won't ever let you go
Cause I want you always
I want you always always

When life gets harder than we planned
I promise I'll listen
I promise I'll do whatever it takes
Cause I, I don't want to waste one single moment
From a silly little mistake"

"I want to give you the world
And all that I have
I want to make you my baby
To have and to hold
I want to give you my word
I'll never let go
I'll never let go

I, I won't give you up
Cause I don't want to live you without you by my side
Forevermore
I want you always
As long as I'm alive
I'll have you 'til the end of time
I won't ever let you go
Cause I want you always

I want you always.

"Legends"

Just a man who never knew his plans included you
Just a man who never knew what wild love could do
Just a man with half a world until your smile crowded in
Just a man whose hand will always guide, protect, and hold you.

Baby boy, your story's just begun
Hold on for the ride, the road's a tragic one
But, baby boy, your story will be legend
Because with the pain comes truth and all that's worth protecting.
Collect the stars, the moon, they're yours for the taking

Baby boy: my heart, my sun, the treasured one
Your time is now, stand tall and sure
There's no mistaking
You're a legend in the making.

ACKNOWLEDGEMENTS

From the start of my journey, I've been blown away by the amount of support from new friends, readers, bloggers, and fellow authors. I can't possibly see this as my accomplishment, but as an incredible blessing thanks, in large part, to all of you. There are so many people in my heart, and I wish I could list every one of you, even though I know it's impossible. Please know that I treasure you all and take nothing for granted.

To my amazing husband who is always there to support me. Without you I would not be writing these words.

To Sunniva Dee and Hazel James: my amazing ABs and CPs. I'm so happy honored to share a brain with people as amazing as you.

To Nicola Tremere: Thank you for being my UK Consultant. Even more importantly, thank you for being such a good friend.

To Lindsey DeCastro: Your friendship and feedback mean so much to me.

To Jon Meckes: As always, thank you for lending your talent and music industry expertise.

To Andy Van Horn: AKA Officer Andy. Thank you for your sharing your law enforcement knowledge and patience for my many questions!

To the "epic" members of ABC (Aly's Breakfast Club): I can never thank you enough for your encouragement and support. You always bring a smile to my face and remind me why I do this. I love you hard!

To all my readers, I wish I could thank every one of you. Thank you for taking this journey with me and I would love to hear from you!

CONTACT ALYSON

Alyson Santos
PO Box 577
Trexlertown, PA 18087-0577

Facebook: Author Alyson Santos
Facebook Reader Group: Aly's Breakfast Club
BookBub
Website: http://www.alysonsantos.com/
Instagram: AuthorAlysonSantos
Book+Main
Spotify: AuthorAlysonSantos
YouTube: Author Alyson Santos
Twitter: AuthorAlySantos

CPSIA information can be obtained
at www.ICGtesting.com
Printed in the USA
BVHW040825080119
537306BV00016B/152/P